D1235220

GUARDING LAUREN

BROTHERHOOD PROTECTORS WORLD

BARB HAN

Twisted Page Press LLC

BROTHERHOOD PROTECTORS

ORIGINAL SERIES BY ELLE JAMES

Brotherhood Protectors Series

Montana SEAL (#1)

Bride Protector SEAL (#2)

Montana D-Force (#3)

Cowboy D-Force (#4)

Montana Ranger (#5)

Montana Dog Soldier (#6)

Montana SEAL Daddy (#7)

Montana Ranger's Wedding Vow (#8)

Montana SEAL Undercover Daddy (#9)

Cape Cod SEAL Rescue (#10)

Montana SEAL Friendly Fire (#11)

Montana SEAL's Mail-Order Bride (#12)

SEAL Justice (#13)

Ranger Creed (#14)

Delta Force Strong (#15)

Montana Rescue (Sleeper SEAL)

Hot SEAL Salty Dog (SEALs in Paradise)

Hot SEAL Hawaiian Nights (SEALs in Paradise)

To Elle James for letting me write in your world and introducing me to your awesome readers—a huge thank you. You already know how much I love you.

CHAPTER 1

THE TEXAS SUN beat down on the white canopy over a fresh grave, creating a greenhouse effect and intensifying triple-digit temperatures.

Jaden Dean loosened his tie.

At five o'clock the heat had peaked. A half hour into the inferno, his shirt threatened to melt into his skin. But his mind was far from the August heat in San Antonio. His focus was Helena Turner.

Long after the few attendees had gone home, she sat there, broken. A stark contrast to the deadly field operative she was. Jaden couldn't walk away, so he moved to the chair next to her. "There anyone I can call?"

She didn't look at him. Only shook her head before staring at a spot across the manicured lawn.

Jaden sighed sharply. "Talk to someone. A priest?"

She didn't respond.

"Then take some time off. Hell, take as much time as you need. I'll work it out with Gunner. Your job will be waiting for you. ManTech can survive without you." As her supervisor Jaden could make that call. He'd clear it with Gunner Randol, the owner of the agency, at their next rally point.

She glanced at Jaden.

Damn, it was hard to look her in the eyes, see the pain there. Pain that was his fault because he'd essentially sent Tim to his death.

"Work is all I have," she admitted.

Right. She'd been orphaned as a child. A wrench tightened inside Jaden's gut at remembering the details of her abusive past. There was no family to surround her. Tim had been everything to her. He was her love. Her redemption. Her life. And now he was dead.

Shame washed over Jaden for allowing Tim to take the assignment that was supposed to be Jaden's. Jaden was the supervising officer. He had more experience. It should've been him in that jungle, not Tim.

Helena's chin shot up. "Whoever is responsible will pay for this."

The hollow look in her eyes was a knife to his chest.

Jaden knew all about losing someone close. The darkness and anger that settled in the soul. The hopelessness.

His operatives were all the family he had. One-by-one they were being killed. He was beginning to think he was cursed.

LAUREN JAMES HAD LEARNED the hard way that sometimes the best childhood was a brief one, there was a direct link between determination and success, and it only took one phone call to unleash hurt and memories she'd spent the past decade trying to suppress.

"Help me," a man's voice choked out. It was strained and cracked. His identity was unmistakable.

"Max—" A crack followed by a pained grunt dropped her stomach to the floor, scrambling her nerves.

"Max. Max? Are you there? Are you hurt? Who's doing this to you?" The words fired off like buckshot. Her brother had called four times in the past three months. She'd ignored all of them because when he'd called four years ago he wanted to use her for money.

Lauren had emptied her savings in order to give him the help he said he desperately needed. She'd followed his instructions. Once the money transfer had been made, Max had promised a stint in rehab before going to work in her small florist business where she specialized in native plants and wildflower arrangements.

It was supposed to be a fresh start for Max. But

he'd disappeared as quickly as her savings. She'd sworn never to be taken advantage of again.

More muffled noises, and then a tortured scream seared her eardrums. This call was different than the others.

"Max?" she asked but no response came.

Three days passed before she got another call from an unidentified number.

"Pay or we cut him into pieces." The male voice was unfamiliar but had a distinct Latin accent.

Icy regret stabbed her chest. Why hadn't she tracked her brother down after the last call? Made sure he was safe?

"No. Don't hurt him. Tell me what to do," she said, trying to keep panic out of her voice. Think. Think. Her cell was in her purse in the kitchen. Could she get to it?

"You bring the feds, young lady, we cut him up and mail you the pieces."

No federal officers. Of course they would have anticipated that.

Scuffling noises came through the line before another loud crack sounded.

"Then we come looking for you."

"No. No law enforcement. I'll be there," she promised.

Max screamed in agony, then shouted, "Don't do it, sis. Don't listen to them. Go far away and don't come back. They'll kill you too. I'm already dead."

Even though she'd promised herself that she would never be pulled into Max's world again, she couldn't turn her back on him. Not like this.

"Please. Stop. Don't hurt him. I'll do whatever you want. I'll go wherever you say. Just tell me what to do."

"You better pay, perra. If you don't want to glue his body parts back together. One hundred and fifty thousand dollars."

Another crack sounded, followed by more moaning.

"Please. Stop. I'll. Do. Anything." She had to find a way. A throb ricocheted between her temples.

"Antigua Bay Resort. In two days. On the beach at noon."

Click.

"Oh. God. No."

Lauren didn't hang up. Not even when the dial tone sounded.

Think. Think. She had a little money in savings. Her business was doing well. Maybe she could secure a loan for the rest? But how? There was no time. Where on earth would she get that kind of cash on short notice?

Knees weak, she sank to the kitchen floor. Her body quaked. A slow ripple that arose deep in her belly moved through her chest, her arms, her fingers.

Tremors vibrated down her legs.

She didn't move. Or cry. The fight drained from her.

But she shook so hard it felt as though her bones might fracture, splinter through her skin, and explode into a thousand tiny flecks of dust.

CHAPTER 2

AN UNTRACEABLE CALL. A hundred-fifty thousand dollar loan. An express ticket to a known money launderer's favorite drop spot. An innocent woman caught in the middle. And the dog really ate your homework, didn't it, sweetheart?

Jaden Dean raked his fingers through jet-black hair, ignoring the icy chill running down his spine as he memorized the details of Lauren James's file while on the flight.

Two weeks had passed since he'd taken the assignment to keep an eye on her. It was supposed to be a simple, local babysitting job while he recovered from his injuries after being shot on his last mission. The Blackwater-type agency he worked for was headquartered in D.C. but Jaden was a Dallas man. He'd be stupid to ignore the similarities between missions.

Jaden had recently been burned by a so-called innocent woman trapped in a sting by a family member. Experience had taught him there was no such thing as straightforward when it came to family ties and criminals. Besides, it had taken some skill to get that amount of money on a flight undetected.

Nothing had been transparent since Tim Johnson's death a little more than a month ago. Tim should be alive. Then a week later, Agent Smith had taken a bullet while on assignment with Jaden, who by all counts should also be dead. Smith was buried six-feet under and Jaden had a permanent reminder of the failed mission in the form of a bullet hole in his shoulder.

They'd been working a mission to gain crucial evidence on the Menendez family so the American government could issue warrants and stop the flood of money and illegal weapons flooding the streets and landing in the hands of a couple powerful gangs in Portland. It was getting more dangerous in the jungle and harder to know who to trust. Jaden should know. Camila Menendez had played him for a fool.

Jaden ran his hand over the stubble on his chin. What the hell was happening? He'd spent the past month trying to figure out exactly when and where he'd gone wrong.

And now everyone had to keep an eye on Helena. She'd been blinded by her grief and was becoming a liability. She was a distraction ManTech couldn't afford.

He picked up Lauren James's picture from the file of intel and studied it intently. Jogging shorts and a tightly-fitted tank revealed flawless ivory skin. Her curly mane of red hair was pulled back into a pony-tail, exposing her bare neck.

Her body? One look at her perfect, long runner's legs said she'd picked the right sport. Her lean, taut body was built for the track. To say she was attractive was a lot like saying a motorcycle had two wheels.

She looked exactly like the kind of woman Jaden would want to get to know better. Except his attrac-tion was out of place under the circumstances.

He stood and stretched long, muscular legs. The memory of his recent encounter with Smith's wife still a little too fresh. Normally, he'd push the memory down deep and create some distance from it. The anguish, the crying, the whole scene had nearly done Jaden in. He did emotion about as well as he did family. His job left room for neither. Smith had mistakenly thought he could have it both ways. He'd left behind a heartbroken wife and two kids in diapers.

The pilot turned on the *Fasten Seatbelt* sign and made an announcement that they were starting their descent. Jaden's shoulders tensed and his chest squeezed. He tried not to think about the fact that he was flying to the Caribbean during hurricane season.

He tucked the picture of Lauren James in the file and closed the folder during landing.

The plane bustled with activity as soon as clearance came for passengers to move around the cabin.

Jaden reached for his bag in the overhead bin. Pain tore through his shoulder centering on the point of the bullet's entry. He cursed as he tightened this grip on the handle, pulled the bag down, and deplaned.

Bryce, his spotter, was already on the ground waiting at the rendezvous site. Immediate radio contact informed Jaden that his asset had taken Burma Road until she reached Dickenson Bay on the northwest corner of the island.

Jaden also learned that Lauren had spent fourteen minutes inside the hotel before setting foot on the sand, which he figured was about how long it would take him to reach the beach and locate Bryce.

He was spot on.

"Love the hat. Nice get-up," Jaden said to Bryce. He wore a straw hat and one of those obnoxiously loud Hawaiian shirts with the requisite beer gut to match. Being loud was sometimes the best way to blend in. It was working, because not one person on the teaming beach gave him a second glance.

"Damn." Bryce clutched his chest. "Why're you always sneakin' up on me like that?"

Jaden quirked a smile. "I didn't."

Instinct had him surveying the area before getting too comfortable. The hotel was shaped in a horseshoe, wrapping around a private piece of white sand beach the size of a football field. He glimpsed metal twinkling in the sunlight from the top window of the building to his left. Another on the right. There were two shooters in the building and three on the ground.

Wasn't exactly afternoon tea with the Queen, but he didn't figure he'd break much of a sweat if anything went down.

Jaden was used to working alone in worse situations. His odds doubled having Bryce as backup.

And yet, a little voice in the back of his head fired off a warning.

"What's wrong with my shirt?" Bryce glanced down at the parrots covering the cotton button down. "What do you have against birds?"

"Nothing. I just didn't want to see every species crammed on one sleeve." Jaden was more of a White V-neck Hanes t-shirt and faded blue jeans guy. His compromise on this trip? Flip-flops.

"I'm like the woodwork. Besides, this one here," Bryce said, pointing in the center of his chest, "is an African gray parrot. Pretty, ain't she?"

"She's friggen Miss America. Too bad there's no sunshine to go with a shirt like that," Jaden said with a wry smile. What was it about sunny places that made grown men want to wear shirts they wouldn't be caught dead using to wash their cars with back home?

Bryce glanced up at the skies. "Hurricane's moving in. Supposed to be a bad one. Wouldn't want to have to stick around here longer than I had to."

"Maybe we'll be outta here by lunch. We figure out what she's doing in the mix and why she's giving money to a cartel, and maybe we find Camilla." Jaden was ready to slap handcuffs on her. Death would be the easy way out.

"I hope. I'm hungry," Bryce said, patting his stomach and planting himself on a beach towel.

The small folder with intel about Lauren James's life pointed toward her innocence. Floral shop owner that specialized in native plants and wildflowers. Successful entrepreneur. Tough childhood, yes, but she'd distanced herself and made good. On the surface, she was someone Jaden could even respect.

Was she a simple small business owner who just happened to be related to an international money launderer? Was she the unfortunate recipient of bad shared genes?

"So it's two against five?" Jaden said, not minding those odds.

"Looks so. For now. More's on the way. I can't hang around for long." Bryce looked glum as he checked his watch. "Our guys should've been here already."

"What? You got a problem with the numbers?"

"Like it better when they're flipped," Bryce said truthfully. "Think this situation's about to blow?"

Jaden rolled his shoulders. "Hard to say." He paused, thinking how it would be nice to have at least one friend to watch a game with sometime. "You know, when this is over, we should grab a beer."

"Sure thing."

Jaden leaned forward until he located the asset. Not like he could miss that shock of long red hair against white sand anyway. In the sun, her hair shimmered like crystals.

She sat on the edge of a bright blue lounge chair in the middle of a hundred yards of oceanfront property. There was beach out in front of her, hotel around her, and a row of palm trees on either side. Her small overnight bag was tucked under the lounger. It was most likely stuffed with cash.

She was beautiful. He didn't need to be any closer than five feet from her to tell that. Her pale green tank pressed against full breasts, a white cotton skirt fell to her calves. Her fiery hair framed an almond-shaped face and brown eyes with gold flecks in them. Her lips were full, pink and kissable...he stopped himself right there. Her lips were none of his damn business. He dismissed the thought as a side effect of going too long without female companionship. Another job casualty.

Besides, all the color had drained from her face,

and she was blinking rapidly. Meant she was anxious. Nervous.

Her folded arms and squared shoulders told him she was ready to jump out of her skin if someone yelled, "Boo." And yet, he had to give it to her, she was being brave enough to sit there anyway. Of course, he couldn't tell if she feared the men watching her or the possibility of getting caught. His initial assessment of her gave him the impression she wasn't a career criminal.

Jaden glimpsed someone moving from around the side of the hotel and heading toward a cluster of palm trees. The man moved stealthily along the row of palms, crouched low enough not to draw attention to himself.

Tension permeated the beach, powering the heat and humidity times ten. Jaden's blood was finally pumping again. Adrenaline. He wouldn't feel this alive sitting behind a desk nursing his shoulder.

The ominous storm clouds that had been threatening thickened as a light sprinkle began. The heavy clouds blocked the sun, making it dark as night. The rain shooed tourists back into the hotel, their fists full of rainbow-colored drinks with chunks of pineapple resting on the rims of the glasses.

Bryce took a step toward Jaden. His eyes bulged, and he made a sharp gasp to force air into his lungs.

Another rush of adrenaline hit Jaden, popping

him to his feet long before his brain had time to register what had happened.

Bryce's large frame stumbled forward, wobbled, and then abruptly sat down. He slumped down. The look of shock was fresh on his face as the African gray parrot on his chest turned blood red. The dark liquid infected every other bird like a strain of H1N1.

Shit.

Bryce was dead.

CHAPTER 3

JADEN TOOK COVER. The beach was too exposed. He couldn't go barreling across it no matter how much his instinct told him he could take the kidnapper with ease. There were too many others covering this stretch of real estate.

At least Jaden had his mark in sight, his own weapon, and the benefit of knowing what he was up against. Knowing your enemy and how many there were created a distinct advantage.

He no longer had the element of surprise on his side. Not since Bryce.

With Lauren thrashing around, Jaden couldn't get a clean shot on the kidnapper. One wrong thrash and there'd be a bullet between her eyes.

He needed her alive.

Where the hell was his backup?

The guy was hauling her toward the parking lot.

Good. Jaden would be covered there. He could move undetected through the cars. He couldn't allow them to take her to a more secure location. They'd be even better prepared there.

He had to make a move now.

Jaden moved quickly around the front side of the hotel. In the lot, there'd be a driver, at least, and probably another gunman. He already knew about the men in the towers. They'd be making their way down to the parking lot by now.

Ignoring the blinding pain in his shoulder, Jaden slipped into the parking lot. He prayed they wouldn't have more shooters upstairs, in the windows, or overlooking the lot.

A quick scan didn't reveal any, but he didn't exactly have time to stick around long enough to get a good read.

He had no idea what Lauren's reaction to him saving her would be. If she fought, that might draw unwanted attention. She could end up compromising her own rescue. He could handle the abductor. He could handle her. He didn't doubt his abilities. He'd become the best by considering every possible angle. She was already in fight or flight mode. He needed to make a mental adjustment for that.

Jaden located the getaway vehicle.

Patience.

The break he was looking for came when he got close enough to see the driver was alone.

The other guy on the beach would have stayed back to sweep the area. He was already to Bryce by now.

Damn. Bryce. Jaden hated leaving him back there on the sand. Everything in his heart made him wat to stay with his colleague in his final moments, not let some asshole criminal drag him off the beach.

Rage heated the blood in his veins to boiling. He tamped down his frustration.

Where were Gunner and the others?

He moved silently through the parking lot, still seething.

Anger always made him think more clearly.

He needed to make a move on the kidnapper before he got Lauren to the vehicle. Patience.

A group of Dumpsters would give him enough clearance to take out the guy unnoticed. Might even buy Jaden the time he needed to snatch Lauren and get her to safety.

Crouched low, he made it to the Dumpsters quickly, quietly, unseen.

He crouched down as they approached. Patience.

She kicked and screamed, despite the kidnapper's hand over her mouth. She had fight in her.

Let them come a little closer.

In one sweeping motion, Jaden snatched them both.

Fists were coming at him hard, as were kicks, but he easily wrestled the South American to the ground.

Lauren was over top of him, slamming her fists into him as he held onto her leg.

"Don't fight me," he growled at her, their gazes holding briefly, while pulling his Glock from the waistband of his jeans. He pressed the cold metal severely against the kidnapper's forehead, the bullet meant for him already loaded in the chamber. "Or I'll shoot you too."

Fear had her golden eyes opened wide, but her jaw was set.

"Help me tie him up," he demanded, pulling his own belt from his jeans and wrapping it around the kidnapper, strapping his arms to his sides.

Lauren hesitated for a split second before she kneeled down and ground her knee into the kidnapper's back.

The guy winced, and then smiled up at her through the pain.

"You won't get away with this, perra," he said through a sneer. A tattoo of an angel covered the left side of his neck.

Lauren balled her fist, reared back, and then slammed it into his face. "That's for Max."

He spit blood.

"Hold on there," Jaden said, surprised. A spray of bullets rained on them from every angle. He'd be amused were it not for the shrapnel flying near his head.

"Get up." Jaden forced the South American to his

feet and pushed him in front of them, figuring she wouldn't mind using this piece of scum as a human shield.

He took Lauren's hand, feeling a sudden spark run between them, and he tucked her behind him.

Pressing the barrel of his gun to the back of the South American's head, Jaden moved them toward the beach. If they could get on the other side of the horseshoe, they could use the building as cover.

The spray of bullets continued from the parking lot. AR-15s? Tactical weapons? Jaden made a mental note and moved on.

It looked as though the gang had regrouped.

A crack of thunder fired overhead. The sky was becoming darker by the second, and there was only one choice—keep moving to the beach.

Jaden kept Lauren tucked safely behind him and the South American in front as he stepped backward toward the surf. The beachgoers were long gone. At least he didn't have to worry about innocent people getting hurt.

Out toward the coastline, he glimpsed a worker bringing in a small dive boat with a handful of tourists who were scattering at the sound of gunfire.

He could make a play for the hotel or get him and Lauren out to sea.

He scanned the area. Five jet skis were to the left. No keys. Those would be at the check-in station a hundred yards away at the palm hut. There were half a dozen kayaks. No good.

The scuba boat offered the best chance to get Lauren and himself away from the heavy artillery moving in their direction.

The man in Jaden's arms went limp, blood squirting from his neck, arms and torso.

"On three, run like hell," he said to Lauren. The man's thin jacket, a Kevlar vest no doubt, was the only reason the two of them were still alive.

"One. Two. *Three.*"

Jaden pushed the body forward and cut around the building, which momentarily blocked the spray of bullets. "They won't stop for long. Move!"

Lauren ran right behind him until they reached the boat where the worker was crouched low, tying off the watercraft. He scanned the boat and saw scuba equipment. Good. That might come in handy later.

Jaden pointed the gun directly at the worker's heart. "We're taking this."

The man put up his hands and half-smiled nervously. "No worries, mon. I'm done with it."

Lauren scrambled onto the watercraft.

"Get down," Jaden commanded, keeping an eye on her as he turned the boat around. She curled up on the floor, hugging her overnight bag and shivering. Fierce as she'd been moments before, now she looked small and out of place. Her white cotton skirt hiked up around her thighs revealing far too much leg for Jaden to completely focus.

What was happening here? He had never allowed himself a moment of distraction on a mission before.

Besides, he'd learned the hard way that looks could be deceiving.

His gut told him she was innocent. Could he trust his instincts with everything going on?

Bryce was dead because of her.

Ominous gray clouds hung in the sky. The air became thick and heavy. The wind picked up. Jaden had bigger problems brewing than a storm. It wouldn't take long for the men chasing them to find a boat or the key to one of those jet skis.

He pulled binoculars from a hook and scanned the coastline.

Damn.

Three manned jet skis had split direction. One to the east. One to the west. And one headed right toward him.

Jaden pressed further out to sea, full throttle, heading south. "Stay down."

A sharp crack split the air. The bullet missed. Jaden pulled his Glock from the waistband of his jeans where he'd tucked it a few minutes ago. "Change of plans. Drive."

Lauren pushed herself upright and fought against heavy winds. As soon as she took the wheel, Jaden aimed and fired.

His shot was a little wide. The jet ski was gaining on them. He made an adjustment for velocity and wind and then fired again. The man on the jet ski flew forward as the watercraft abruptly halted.

He surveyed the water. The other assholes were out of sight. Taking back the wheel, he reached into his pocket for his cell. If he'd kept the boat inside of fifteen miles of shore, give or take, he might be able to grab a signal even through the clouds and rain. It was a stretch. Yet with fewer obstructions on the water, the signal could bend over the horizon a bit.

Besides, using his encrypted cell was the safest way to signal his agency for a pick up.

He checked for bars and got nothing.

"Get back down. Just in case," he said to Lauren.

She immediately dropped to the floor and curled into a ball.

The radio on board worked. He sighed sharply. Everyone and their cousin would be monitoring communications. The Coast Guard and his agency would be good things. The men with guns chasing them, not so much.

Filing the thought, he turned up the radio volume and switched to channel sixteen. He listened before transmitting.

"Aunt Betty heard you come in late for curfew last night," came through a few beats later. "You wanna explain where you were?"

He recognized Helena's voice immediately. What

was she doing on the frequency? She was asking if he could give his coordinates. No. He couldn't. He didn't like using VHF. Not even in code. He felt too exposed. Plus, he didn't want her involved.

"Party got crashed. Nothing is ever as it seems when South Americans show up," he said.

"So true," she acknowledged and her tone was laced with bitterness.

"Have to make sure my date makes it home." All he had to do was stay on long enough for Helena to locate him and not a second longer. The cartel spent almost as much money on monitoring equipment as the Department of Defense. Luckily, research and development at the DOD kept them one step ahead. Barely.

"I'm coming to get you," she said.

"No. We lost another man today. I won't lose you, too. Stay put. I'll keep you informed."

"Can't." The determination in her voice spoke volumes about her intent. She could wind up compromising the mission in order to find the man who killed Tim. There was no way Jaden could convince her to back off. He'd have to make a mental adjustment for that. Yet, including her was too risky. She was too emotionally invested. Loose threads.

Time was running out on the call.

The cartel had sure as hell gone to a lot of trouble to pick up Lauren.

Why?

CHAPTER 4

Lauren looked harmless enough, curled up in a ball in the hull. Her lip quivered even when she put on a brave face. Jaden reminded himself of the expression that said looks could kill. In his profession, they usually did.

"Keep your date heading south," came over the frequency. "The weather isn't cooperating."

Away from shore? "Affirmative."

"Gabriel just handed me a note. Sunnyside vacation reps are waiting at the open house. What does it mean?"

Hell if he knew. He had to think. It was code to keep Helena from figuring out where he should go. Gabriel knew her mental state. Good. But what was he trying to say? Sunnyside? What did that mean? Vacations were taken by the sea. Reps? How did they play into it? Reps with an open house. He got it. Real estate. Condos. Seaside Condos. A safe house.

Jaden couldn't risk waiting longer. He turned off the radio, and smashed it using the fire extinguisher on board.

Lauren recoiled and gasped. "Why'd you do that?"

"To protect us. Why'd you come here?" He turned his attention to her. Experience had taught him she wouldn't tell the truth, but he could tell a lot about her by the lies she told.

Shaking off the confusion and shock, she sat up. "Who are you? And I don't know those people."

"I'm Jaden Dean. I'm part of a private security firm called ManTech," he said, thumping the fuel dial as it floated, keeping his compass pointed south.

"Why are you here?" she asked.

"It's my job."

She clucked her tongue disapprovingly. "To do what? Find me, or arrest me?"

"Keep an eye on you and document who you speak to and meet." That was supposed to be it. Follow the chain and report back to Gunner.

"*You* nearly got us killed back there." She sat upright and crossed those long runner's legs, tugging her skirt below her knees.

"I just saved your life. Or maybe you hadn't noticed you were being dragged to your death?"

She stared out at the seas for a long moment saying nothing. "They might have been taking me to my brother. Are you going to use me to get back at them?" The disdain in her voice was palpable.

"No. I'm the good guy."

A disgruntled snort escaped her. "I can decide that for myself. Is someone paying you to watch me?"

"I get paid to do my job."

"Who hired you?" she shot back.

"I can't tell you what I don't know," he said honestly. Even so, he didn't like the mistrust in her eyes. He couldn't say he blamed her. The simple truth was he didn't know. His contacts were clean. This assignment had come from a big shot in D.C. Not that he would share that tidbit. Several of his men were dead, and this cartel seemed to be the link.

Still, for some unknown reason, it mattered to him that she trusted him. He told himself this would go a lot smoother if he won her confidence and that was all. "What's in the overnight bag?"

"Money."

"If you don't know those guys, why'd you bring a bag full of cash to the beach?" he asked.

"I had no choice." She stared at him, her pupils dilated from adrenaline and fear. "If you're so good at your job, why don't you know already?"

He compressed his lips to keep from popping off with a remark.

"How much trouble is my brother in?" she asked.

He'd swear he just saw her tense expression become laced with anger and bitterness.

"He's been one of the top money launderers in North America for the last couple of years."

"I didn't know." Hurt darkened her eyes as she took a moment for that news to sink in. The catch in her voice had him doubting his initial judgment. Had this information taken her by surprise?

"You do now."

"I thought maybe he was still into drugs," she confessed.

Maybe she told the truth. Maybe she was as devastated as she looked. Maybe she did love her brother and she was just that demolished by him. A little piece of him believed in her integrity. The whole rest of him, and especially the part which had been betrayed, railed against the idea of trusting anyone.

Not that it mattered. Sticking with her would lead him to the men who'd killed Bryce. Lauren James had just found herself a new best friend. And this would all go a lot smoother if she trusted him.

"Sometimes you want to believe in people." He shook his head wearily. "They can be damn disappointing, can't they?"

Her expression solemn, she said, "You radioed your agency before. Are they coming to pick us up?"

"Yes. But we have to get to a safehouse first," he stated.

"Back there I saw a man get shot. Were the two of you close?"

"This job doesn't allow for many friends if that's what you're asking." He paused, not wanting to reveal just how much it hurt to say that. "Why'd you bring the briefcase?"

"To exchange for my brother's life." Her voice trembled in anger. "He's here...*somewhere.* Are you taking me to find him?"

They could re-engage on the south side of the island, and then he could set up a meeting with Gunner for more men and supplies. There were only a few spots on the island where the cartel could be holding her brother. "You're vacation ends when we hit dry land."

"You think I like this? You think I want any of this?" Frustration had her blinking back tears and her voice quivering as a look of repulsion crossed her face. If pressed, Jaden would have to admit he didn't like being the one who put it there.

"They're going to kill my brother now, and it's because of you," she said.

"Just how do you figure that?"

"They told me to bring money to buy him back. That's what I was doing. Until you came along and messed it up." She folded her arms across her chest.

"Unless being kidnapped and probably killed was part of your plan, then you should be glad I ruined it, sweetheart," he said. "Besides, we'll find them."

∼

"How? How on earth will we do that out here?" Lauren's eyes were intent on the man in front of her.

He glanced at the bag.

"They get the money?" His voice was dark, edgy and commanding. No question he was used to being the one in control.

"No."

"Then they'll find us. Besides, your brother's still alive." His confidence was a little shocking under the circumstances and she was caught off guard by how much of a pull it was.

"How could you possibly know that?"

A slow smile spread across lips far too full for a face of sharp planes and hard angles. "This is not my first rodeo."

"Why would you help him? *Me*? Is that why you were hired?"

"I catch bad guys for governments and private agencies. It's what I do," he said.

This was his job. He was a professional. That she knew. What she couldn't figure out was if he would help her or hurt her. She wasn't sure if she should fight him or thank him.

Best she could figure was he'd just saved her life. It was the first time in years someone had come to her rescue and taken care of her. And it felt nice to know someone had her back—a dark knight with sex appeal in buckets. She couldn't deny the flicker of attraction she'd felt the second she set eyes on him. But, he was the one with the gun.

"Thank you for helping me earlier," she finally said.

"We're safe," he said. "For now."

"What's going to happen to my brother?" She hated the quiver in her voice.

A thump threw her forward. Panic gripped her as the engine ku-clunked before dying.

"What was that?" she asked.

His hands went to work on the controls. "A bad sign."

The engine whirred but didn't catch. He picked up the binoculars and scanned the area. "We can't stay here. You know how to swim?"

"Yes."

"In the ocean?" he asked.

"There a difference?" she shot back.

"In the water, your clothes will turn to lead weights in a matter of minutes. I have no idea how long we'll be swimming. But I'm certain of two things. Stay here and you'll die. Wear those and you'll drown."

His shirt was off and crumpled on the floor. His muscled chest glistened from the light rain as he dug around in the scuba gear. He examined a wetsuit. "This should be the right size for you."

He tossed the material toward her.

She shot him a look. "You expect me to put this on right here?"

"You see a dressing room?"

"Fine. Then turn around," she said stiffly, before turning to face opposite him.

"Nothing I haven't seen before, sweetheart."

Feeling more vulnerable than she wanted to admit, she slipped off her pale green tank top. The tiny hairs on the back of her neck pricked as she slid her skirt down past her hips and turned just in time to catch Jaden boldly staring at her.

Breath stalled in her throat. She stepped out of her skirt. Her heart thudded against her ribcage.

"I told you not to look." She covered herself with the wetsuit.

He grinned a devastating little grin, saying nothing.

"Besides, how do I know you're not working for one of those jerks?"

He stepped closer, using his large frame to crowd her against the side of the boat. "You really think I'm the kind of man who does other people's dirty work?"

She jolted at the nearness of his voice. He was so close now she could smell the woodsy scent of his aftershave. For the first time she was keenly aware of just how tall he was. He had to be at least six-feet-three, maybe more. Standing this close to her, he nearly dwarfed her frame at five-feet-four.

"No." She didn't think that. If Jaden Dean had dirty work to do, he did it for himself. "I don't know what kind of man you really are."

"You don't need to." He didn't lack confidence and maybe that was part of the draw to him.

"If you're trying to scare me," she said, "it won't work."

"I supposed you're not trembling, either."

Frustration shot through her, because damn it, he was right. Refusing to give an inch, she shot back, "I'm cold."

"Try again."

CHAPTER 5

With shaky fingers she zipped her wetsuit. Thank God he'd turned back to the pile of equipment, no doubt searching for anything useful. She needed a second to pull it together and calm her rattled self.

"I never could figure this thing out." She hated how uneven her voice sounded as she pointed to her buoyancy control vest.

"Tighten it here." He moved closer, his tone dropping an octave. His finger brushed across her stomach, causing heat to swirl low in her belly. "Should be snug across here but not too tight under the arms."

Lauren slipped on her weight belt, followed by her tank, ignoring the sensations igniting her nervous system from his slightest touch. He was dark and dangerous, and he'd just saved her life. Her body was simply reacting to that. "I don't know anything about you aside from your name."

"No. You don't." he tanked up without breaking rhythm; his gruff tone suggested they were done talking. "If you want to stay alive, you'd better follow me."

She clutched her overnight bag.

"You can't swim with that."

Panic widened her eyes. "This is everything I have. There's no more. I told you. If I don't bring this my brother's dead. I have to—"

"You give them that and it's game over, you die." As if to punctuate his sentence, Jaden picked up his gun and fired off a round into the water, emptying the chamber, and then tossed the clip overboard before securing his gun back inside his wetsuit.

"What did you just do?" she asked.

"Bullets on a Glock and water don't mix," was all he said. Then came, "and I'm serious about losing the bag."

Lauren flinched as she set it down, cleared her throat, and positioned herself on the edge of the boat, preparing for the backward spiral into the water. The sound of an engine roared in the distance. Panic gripped her. The men were getting closer.

If they got the money, would they kill Max?

"Hold on." She grabbed the fire extinguisher, tied it onto her piece of luggage, and tossed it overboard. "This might buy Max a little more time if they find the boat."

Standing there, watching her life savings sink into the water, her heart seized.

Jaden nodded approvingly, and that same heart stuttered. She shouldn't care what this man thought.

She reclaimed her seat and noticed that the vessel was taking on water. Normally, the water in the Caribbean was like glass, providing a clear view to the sand below, but the storm-churned seas had her diving in blind.

She leaned back, splashed into the water and then righted herself in order to swim.

When they'd gone a great distance, thumbs up, Jaden gave the signal to ascend.

Waves broke over her head. Rain came down in buckets, dropping visibility down to a few feet. All she could see was water.

"What's going on?" She had to shout to be heard over the howling wind, terror vibrating her tone.

Jaden raked his fingers through his hair. "We'll figure something out."

Rolling, dark clouds swelled overhead and panic caused her heart to thump wildly.

"Inflate your BC." His voice was controlled, providing a small measure of comfort while Lauren was freaking out.

"Right." Good idea. Her buoyancy control device would make her float, keeping her on top of the water without her wasting valuable energy. Lauren located the knob and squeezed the inflator button a couple of bursts. She pushed her legs forward, flattened her back, and allowed herself a moment to get her bearings.

"I probably shouldn't even care. I mean, I know what he is." She didn't respect her brother. How could she? But he hadn't always been like this.

"He was my hero when we were kids. He saved me from a lot of bad things." He'd done so much for her. Why couldn't she save him back?

Jaden's expression changed as he studied her. He seemed to pick up on the implication she made. His pupils dilated as though angry and his lips thinned. "He saved you from things or people?"

"People. It's the real reason I came here." Compared to young Max, Superman was just a silly-looking guy in a cape.

A moment of silence sat between them.

"Don't worry. We'll get to him. I promise." Jaden's hand went up, his expression set with more determination than ever. "The direction of the wind should help blow us ashore—"

"Which way is that?"

Jaden pointed, seemed sure of himself, but how he could tell was anybody's guess.

A sinking feeling swelled inside Lauren's stomach.

At least her wetsuit provided some measure of insulation against the elements. But without the sun, even seventy-degree water caused a chill to goose bump both of her arms in her short-sleeved wetsuit.

Jaden set his jaw. "We can swim at right angles to the wind to bring us closer to shore."

"How far is that?" Lauren wasn't sure she wanted the answer to that question. The chilly wind was already causing a reaction in her body. Her nerves were shot. Adrenaline wore thin.

"Hard to tell."

Maybe he didn't want to say.

"I need you to trust me. We'll be okay."

Trust?

Lauren couldn't remember the last time she'd believed in someone else.

RANDOM THOUGHTS CAME into Jaden's head as he swam. Not of dying though, despite the circumstances. The water wasn't too cold. The real struggle was to keep morale up. Keep Lauren moving forward. Once they got to safety, they'd retrieve her brother and Jaden would send them both home. Case closed.

When she'd told him her brother had saved her from bad people—and by people he instantly knew she meant men—rage flared inside him at the thought that someone might have hurt her. His protective instincts jumped to high alert and he wanted her to know he would never hurt her.

It was a promise he knew he couldn't keep.

Similar to the beers he and Bryce had committed to having back there on the beach.

Jaden's line of work didn't allow for keeping promises. Ask Smith's wife. Or Helena.

Guilt knifed his chest.

This was an assignment. It was his job to watch over Lauren and find out if she was involved with her brother. She was an asset. He shouldn't let her get inside his head.

Checking his watch, he realized they'd been swimming well over an hour.

Her spirits were sagging, and keeping them up until they reached safety would be the bigger challenge. Not to mention the fact that the longer they stayed in the ocean, the closer that hurricane would get. They needed to get out before conditions worsened. Jaden could see Lauren was trying to put up a brave front. It stirred a place deep inside him.

Not that it nattered now, she was getting weak. He needed to maintain focus.

As Jaden pulled a torch and scanned the surface, he located ridges jutting out of the water. "Over there. Rocks." He pointed. A break would give Lauren time to regroup. They couldn't stay long.

Up close, the island looked more like headstones flagging a watery grave.

But then, there were worse things to be afraid of than death.

Lauren's voice broke through as she pointed

directly at him. She must've found a rock, or the base of the incline. Panic etched lines in her face, the whites of her eyes the only things glowing in the ever-darkening sky.

"A wave!" she shouted.

Jaden forced himself to face forward as water tugged at him from behind, meaning one thing—a huge swell pulled him backward.

Jaden scrambled on top of the surf, looked up in time to see he was being pulled away from Lauren. The rain was coming down hard, and he struggled to focus his eyes. If anything happened to him, Lauren would be alone. Defenseless. On a freaking rock. Anger balled up and lodged in his chest.

Rain pounded on the water, causing salt to splash up and burn his eyes. He was getting close as he strained to get a good look. There she stood. Dripping with water in the haze of rain between them, he could see her silhouette.

Her gasp echoed through driving rain. Jaden glanced up as a huge swell sucked him back.

Completely consumed by the swell, an explosion of energy burst through Jaden's chest, vibrating to the ends of his body.

Then darkness.

PAIN RIFLED through Jaden's legs and up his spine

until his entire body ached to the point of constant, dull throbbing. He shifted on the rock. Rain pelted his cheeks as the wind howled. He squinted. A fog thicker than the storm clouds overhead clouded his mind. He couldn't focus.

What had happened?

A memory cut through his mind's haze in the way a fin slices waves. A stab of pain. His knee. Pain aside, all his body parts seemed to be in order. He remembered slamming into a rock.

He squinted an eye open through the burn.

Lifting his head brought blinding pain to his neck as both hands went to his face, and he used the butts of them to hammer his forehead. A salty, dry coating covered his tongue.

He recalled the wave. It probably had slammed his leg into a rock.

And Lauren. Where was Lauren? He had to find her.

Damn it. He'd known it was a risky move using the radio back on the boat. The cartel had most likely pinpointed their location because of the transmission and that move had cost them their boat.

He needed to get a message to Gunner to let his boss know that he was safe. The boat they'd used earlier was most likely at the bottom of the sea by now.

A wild thought struck. Could someone inside the agency have given away his position? The same mole that had cost Tim and Smith their lives? Considering every possibility was habit even though he feared he was becoming too cynical. This job was beginning to weigh on him.

Stretching out his foot and groaning from pain, he heard a hammering sound bite through the howling wind. What was that? A plane. No. A chopper. Sounded like a chopper.

He popped to his feet, but his bad knee gave and landed him hard on his backside. His people would be scouting the seas for him by now.

"Here! Down here!" he shouted, the words bouncing off the thick clouds above and back down to him.

Ignoring the pain, he shouted again as he patted himself down looking for another flare. He'd had two but found nothing.

The roar of the engine faded.

By now, the chopper was too far. A flare wouldn't help. He railed against the urge to spew out another round of swear words. Besides, what good would it do? He'd still be hurt. Stranded.

Damn.

His best chance to get to safety had disappeared into the clouds.

Thunder clapped in the sky.

What the hell happened to Lauren? The thought of her lying somewhere bleeding racked his insides.

A quick scan of the area provided no reassurances, no sign of her.

Out of the corner of his eye, Jaden caught something move by a nearby boulder.

He scrambled to his feet but couldn't make out what was bobbing up and down in the water.

CHAPTER 6

"THANK GOODNESS YOU'RE ALIVE," Lauren said, looking relieved as she rounded the corner, rushing to get closer to Jaden.

He couldn't admit to himself just how happy seeing her made him and it was more than just for work reasons. Her intelligence, determination and devotion to her family had hit him in a place he thought long dead. Her beauty only added to the equation. "Seems that way."

"I was so worried when I couldn't wake you," she admitted. The concern in her eyes—concern for him —was another thing he shouldn't allow to bring light into that dark place inside his soul.

Taking a step forward, his foot slipped on loose rocks. He caught the top of a big boulder to steady himself. His dry mouth reminded him dehydration was swallowing him, all the water around a constant reminder of an insatiable thirst. Nothing fit to drink. His stomach was tight, queasy. He could only imagine how torn up he must look, especially if his insides were any kind of gauge.

"Sit down," she urged.

"How'd you get me here?" He opened his mouth and tried to catch raindrops on his tongue to ease the dryness, still unable to admit to himself how much his heart danced from the sight of her.

"I managed," she said.

"Are you crazy, coming after me like that?" She must've dragged him out of the water and fifteen feet away from the edge.

"What choice did I have? You saved my life, remember? It was the least I could do for you. Besides, you're bleeding." More of that concern came through but he looked away before it could seed.

Leaning back, he summed up his injuries as nothing more than a few scratches. "Not bad."

"You won't be walking for a while."

"This? No. I'm fine. A few scrapes." He brought his hand to his forehead, wincing in pain as the movement dulled his aching body. If he were honest, the sight of her calmed more than his physical aches and pains. But that was ridiculous. They'd barely met.

Still, for half a second he wondered if she felt the emotion tethering them together with an invisible electric line as much as he did. The charges of electricity that came with it? He needed to get the conversation on the right track. "Did anything stand out with Max's phone call? Do you recall any noise in the background?"

"Wait, I heard a train when they called. Wherever they were hiding him must've had a track nearby," she said. "Do you think he's even on the island?"

"I hope so."

LAUREN LEANED in to get a better look at Jaden's face. Again, Jaden winced as he moved and Lauren guessed his injuries were worse than he wanted to admit.

"You need rest." For a brief moment her gaze flickered from his eyes to his lips...for a split second she saw an image of those lips pressed against hers. This was not the time for an inappropriate fantasy. Besides, he was injured. And they were stranded.

"How bad is the pain?" she asked.

His broad shoulders rolled, his expression tensed as he moved, showing he was unwilling to own up to his true amount of pain.

"We have to get out of here soon." He glanced up at the sky.

"Not until you can move." She moved to a neatly stacked pile before returning a moment later with a wadded up piece of cloth, which she touched to his forehead to blot the blood.

"Ouch." He jerked back as his hand closed tightly on hers.

"Sorry. The salt." She wrung out the piece of material one more time before touching it to the gash on his arm, afraid to acknowledge to herself how strong her physical attraction was to a stranger. She chalked it up to the fact that he'd saved her life countless times already.

Blotting the cut, she did her best to conceal just how frantic she'd been moments before, when she didn't know if he'd break consciousness. Maybe it was the circumstances, but she wanted to know more about this man, be closer to him. She told herself her interest in him didn't go any deeper than needing to know if she could really trust him. The notion was foreign. Lauren didn't trust anyone. "How does it feel?"

"Hurts. Hard to tell what hurts the most though." He issued a dry crack of a smile. "It's nothing a good night of sleep won't cure."

Good that he could joke under the circumstances.

He gestured toward the rocks. "Find anything we can use?"

"Not much. It's pretty barren," she admitted, tamping down the hopeless feeling trying to engulf her. They were stranded in the ocean on a bed of rocks in a storm.

"See real land anywhere?" he asked.

"Thought I saw something over there." Jaden's gaze followed where she pointed.

He glanced up at the sky. "Doesn't look good for us to stick around here any longer than we have to."

"The rain comes and goes. I'm more worried about you, though," she said honestly.

"I'll live." He stretched out his leg and laid his head back on a rock before closing his eyes. He brought his hand up to touch her arm, rippling volts of electricity through her. Before her body could launch a full-on assault she blinked and scooted back, refusing to be taken in by those perfect blue eyes.

"What is it you do when you're not saving women from scary men and dangers in the water?" She'd almost died today. That would get anyone's blood pumping

"I told you."

Right. Secret security agency. That would explain those muscles.

"Doing what exactly?" she pressed.

"Things I can't talk about."

"Don't want to, or can't?" She tilted her head to one side, her curiosity was starting to run wild.

He didn't respond.

"Why are you really looking for me? I have no secrets, and the government can't possibly care about my life. You think I'm involved with my brother?" she said incredulously.

He seemed to contemplate that for a moment.

"You were a glorified babysitting job until you took out that loan and bought a ticket to the Caribbean."

It was high time she knew exactly where she stood. They were stranded out to sea. He was her only hope of survival. "You *do* think I'm involved."

"Not anymore."

"I hate those scumbags worse than you do." She raged against the tears threatening. A few tumbled and rolled down her cheeks anyway, salty as the cursed seas. She told herself she was angry at her brother for not being stronger, for not leaving that horrible childhood they'd had behind, for not doing as she had and refusing to let it ruin his life. All of this had nothing to do with Jaden's accusations.

"Not possible." A flash of darkness moved behind his eyes. "Then tell me more about Max. What's your involvement with him?"

She heaved a sigh. "I should know about my own brother. But I don't. I didn't know about his illegal activities until you told me."

"You had no idea before now?"

"I knew he was using drugs and had gotten himself into trouble before. We haven't spoken in years." Her voice cracked at the end of her sentence.

"Why's that?" he asked.

She glared at him. "Isn't it obvious?"

"Look, I got a dead man back on the beach who should be alive right now." His voice was laced with anger and guilt.

"Which is an interesting point," she said.

"Meaning?" he asked.

"Where's your cavalry?" She glanced up at the sky when he didn't respond. "Your job teach you anything about weather?"

"I've seen a lot of storms." He nodded.

"Any chance this'll pass?"

"I'd hoped." His voice was filled with dread. "See those large, rounded puffs of clouds covering the sky with a grayish veil? Always comes before the weather gets worse."

"Great." Things could actually get worse?

"You're cold." His hand closed on Lauren's arm, sending shivers up it, and she felt herself being drawn toward him.

She pulled back immediately.

Clutching at her wetsuit, she hopped to her feet.

He grabbed her ankle, stopping her from taking a step while the pain of movement caused his face to crinkle. "Look. I'm outta line."

She should've felt anger, and she did, but she also felt her pulse rise and sensual tingles skitter across her skin. She cleared her throat like that might get rid of them.

He pulled her closer. "Our body heat will warm us both."

His touch caused her nerve endings to quiver and her senses to kick on high alert. Her gaze dropped to his broad chest, and she watched as it rose and fell in rhythm with hers.

"I shouldn't—"

"Hold on, sweetheart. You're shivering. It's the best I can do."

Looking out onto the surf, she was utterly dumbstruck. Because angry as she might be, she couldn't ignore the fact that she'd felt none of those pounding feelings inside when other men had touched her. She'd never reacted to anyone's touch the way she did with this man's.

Numb from such an overload of emotions descending on her, she didn't fake a smile. Instead, Lauren clamped her lips and held back the urge to kiss him. She forced her thoughts to her brother. "I didn't ask for any of this. I hope you know that."

"Innocent people rarely ever do." A grimace took hold of his expression. Jaden's arm went around her shoulders. "You're shivering."

She ignored the spark of fire from his touch and scanned the skies. Blackness everywhere. No hope for a break in sight. "If you're feeling better, shouldn't we get going?"

"As soon as I stop bleeding."

"Where?" She'd been so focused on keeping her emotions in check she'd momentarily forgotten about his injuries.

"Here." He pointed toward his shoulder. "And

there." He motioned toward multiple cuts on his right shin.

Thunder clapped in the sky directly overhead. A fierce reminder there wasn't much time to regroup.

"Let me see what I can do for your cut." Quickly, she moved to the pile of supplies she'd gathered and then back. "I can make a bandage with this."

She couldn't steady her hands being so near to Jaden, unsure if it was anger or something else entirely. And she nearly dropped the torn piece of clothing she was holding. "Close your eyes."

It would help if his intense blue eyes weren't staring directly at her.

He leaned his head back on a rock as he winced. "And how is it that you know how to do this?"

She went to work placing the scrap of material on his cut and tying it with the straps. "You grow up like I did and you learn to do plenty for yourself."

Too much, probably. Lauren had never been able to allow herself to rely on anyone else.

"That why you came to help your brother?" he asked.

"Not that it's your business but, yes. He came to my rescue when one of my mom's 'dates' decided he'd take what he wanted from her fourteen-year-old daughter while said mother was passed out."

Every muscle in Jaden's body tensed as she pulled the strap closed.

"Sorry. I'm hurting you," she said meeting his

gaze. His shifted from hers, skipped over her breasts to the makeshift Band-Aid she'd fashioned on his hand.

Being so close to Jaden caused her pulse to pound in her veins and her body to spark, reacting to the sexual chemistry. And here she knew nothing about him. What was it about this guy that was getting to her?

Maybe that was the attraction. A strong mystery man who'd swooped in to save her like a superhero. A real-life good guy.

Who wouldn't be attracted to that?

"Let me warm you up." He bent further until he could wrap his strong arms around her and pull her up until she was kneeling inside his thighs. Her hips were inches from his skin. Heat pulsed between them.

"You're exhausted, aren't you?" He brushed back her hair and really looked at her. There was a hint of vulnerability in those determined eyes.

The weather had turned.

She sensed he knew it, too.

Lauren grabbed hold of his waist, not so much as a conscious decision as just raw instinct, basking in the warmth his body provided for another moment.

A thin layer of mesh kept her naked skin from his bare chest.

Reminding herself that he'd likely saved her life back there in the water, again, she decided her attraction to him was really gratitude, nothing more.

And what did it matter? No matter how strong her feelings for him were at the moment, they wouldn't last. Lauren didn't do 'close.' Not since her mother. Not since her brother. Not since opening up to her young and handsome English professor who'd made her believe in the redemptive power of love until she got a nasty phone call from his wife. Jerk.

She regained her senses and stood up.

CHAPTER 7

THE WINDS KICKED up to a cacophony of lightning flashes against the backdrop of heavy clouds and thunder.

Thunder cracked as a lightning bolt raced sideways across the sky. Jaden's ears rang, his head pounded. Lauren's wide golden eyes threatened to fracture the emotional wall he'd built.

The air was heavy and thick.

Jaden crouched down at the edge of the water, thinking that he'd never been around another person who retreated quicker than Lauren. The moment he tried to get close, she'd back away. The best and only thing he could do was to give her space.

She moved beside him. He angled his face toward her and studied her.

"I'm sorry about the way I acted a few minutes

ago," she said. "I don't know what it is about being with you that scares me."

He must've made a face because she quickly added, "I'm not afraid of you. I don't think you're going to hurt me. There's something about being around you, a pull, attraction, whatever you want to call it that catches me off guard. I've never felt this so strongly before and I'm pretty certain today might be my last on this earth. So, if it's okay with you I want you to kiss me."

Awareness shot through Jaden as he looked into her eyes and saw a dangerous mix of hunger and need there. He brought his hands up to cradle her face and tilt her chin toward him, drawing her lips near his. "This is a bad idea."

"I don't really care right—" The rest of the words were silenced when his mouth crushed hers. She parted her lips for him, and his tongue delved deep.

Heat and a shot of overwhelming need warmed rocketed through him.

He broke off the kiss far too soon when thunder rumbled, shaking the ground.

"Still don't care?" he asked.

She didn't answer because she had to have felt it, too. The two of them together would be an all-consuming fire that neither could afford. She couldn't let herself trust anyone any more than he could.

Jaden refocused.

The swells had momentarily lightened up. Good. The winds were fairly calm. Better. He scanned the water. No fins. Didn't necessarily mean no sharks.

From his position he saw a white object bobbing up and down with the waves. Jaden checked his leg. No blood. Good. Sharks were drawn to blood. The makeshift bandage she'd made had stopped the bleeding.

"Hold on." Wading waist-high, he counted the waves, and on three dove into one. Somewhere in the back of his mind he heard her protests about getting in the water again.

He broke the surface and squinted, trying to get a better look at the mystery article. He didn't have to swim long before reaching it. A wind surfing board. Looked to be in decent condition and like it would hold his weight. This would keep them out of the water and insulate them against dangers lurking there.

Jaden planted his gaze on Lauren with laser precision as he paddled toward her. It didn't take long to return to the rocky coast. He rolled off the board and examined it properly.

"Not bad. The rig and the sail have been ripped clean off though. Still, it should work."

"Are we really supposed to leave on that?" She looked him up and down like he'd lost his mind.

He glanced up at the sky, at the darkening clouds, and said, "We have to go now."

"Okay."

JADEN SLIPPED on his facemask and tucked his fins under his arm. He put on his belt and stuffed the small items inside pockets. "All we have room to carry is a whistle and your fins. It isn't much."

All Lauren's hopes of survival rested on a ten-foot-long piece of foam and a man she barely knew. The last part didn't seem as true as it might've when they'd first ended up on the rocky island.

But what she truly knew about him, his life, could fit in a thimble.

She followed his lead, climbing on the front of the board as he'd instructed.

It felt like she'd been swimming for hours when she caught her first glimpse of land.

Lauren pumped her arms until the board crested the wave again for what seemed like the hundredth time. At that height, she caught another glimpse of the mainland.

"Did you see that?" she shouted back to him against wind gusts that made rain pelt her face.

Another wave crashed down hard, and Lauren spun off the board. She swallowed a mouthful of saltwater, gagging. It burned the back of her throat and nose as she struggled to break the surface.

The surf churned her around as if caught during the Pamplona Bull Run in Spain.

When the wave released, she reached bottom, and then crawled up on all fours pushing forward without opening her eyes. Another swell crashed on top of her and churned her upside-down. Oh, God. Max. What would happen to him now? She wouldn't survive, and he'd be killed. Her head pounded.

Jaden had said he'd save her brother. Why did words from a complete stranger offer so much comfort?

The board rolled, she took a face full of water up her nose and in her mouth. And then everything went black.

JADEN FOUGHT THE RUSHING TIDE. He'd hit bottom. Sand chugged up his nose, in his mouth, his eyes. He coughed up saltwater, shook his head, and tried to get his bearings. He squinted through burning eyes.

The beach.

They were on the beach. Fatigue dragged him down like a shark pulling its prey under water. He rolled onto his side and wiped the sand from his face. Visibility sucked. He couldn't be sure which shore they'd landed on, or if cartel waited nearby.

Lauren.

Where was she?

There. Not three feet away. She didn't amount to more than a lump in the surf. His chest tightened. Nothing could happen to her. *To his asset,* he corrected. She didn't move. He could barely make out her face. His gut tensed, his neck muscles strained. She had to be okay. For the sake of this mission. The cartel wanted her. He needed to figure out why. In keeping her close, he held the chips.

"Lauren." His voice came out as a croak, his throat sore from choking on saltwater. The next thing Jaden knew, the surf crashed on top of him again, yanking him back toward the sea. He crawled toward shore, sat straight up, and then did a quick check for signs of more injuries. Legs looked okay. Muscles ached, and he was more tired than when he'd come off a three-month assignment in the jungle, but he was intact. He crawled to Lauren. She was folded over on her side, her chest slightly moving.

He felt for a pulse, got one, and then gently shook her.

Her eyes blinked open. Closed quickly. An inch-long gash scored her forehead above her right eyebrow. Blood pulsed from it.

"You're gonna be okay, you hear me?" He couldn't even think of what he'd do if something bad happened to her. A vise grip squeezed his chest when she didn't budge.

He sure didn't plan to leave her out there. No amount of pain would stop him from taking her to the emergency safe house. If they'd landed on the south side of the island as he suspected, Gregory would be waiting at Beachside Condos. Jaden couldn't get a message to his contact with a dead cell. He hoped like hell Gregory would be ready for them.

Jaden lumbered to his feet and scooped Lauren up. He couldn't see more than twenty feet in either direction. Chinks of debris flew past his head. If the winds had seemed harsh at sea, they'd more than doubled in velocity on the beach. Moving her out of the surf, he gently lay her down. He hated the thought of leaving her, even for a minute, while looking so defenseless. Damn it.

Leaning closer, he cupped her face in his hands. Her once bright eyes were fading. "I'll be right back." He planted a kiss on her lips.

She didn't so much as blink.

Nothing on the beach looked familiar, not that he could see far. He battled to orient himself. Suddenly the fact that the island had three hundred and sixty-five beaches sent a jolt down his spine. Jesus, how could he figure out where they were?

They could be on any one of them—not to mention sand was flying everywhere, blurring his vision and burning his eyes.

He coughed up the little crystals that had flooded every orifice.

Turning his back to the sea, he jogged toward palm trees, ignoring the frustration tightening in his chest. Lauren had to be all right. He would find safety. There would be no other choice.

His hands fisted at the thought of the cartel getting to her before he got back. They get to her, and his trail would run cold. But it was more than business that had him needing to take care of her.

Luckily, the beach was small. Just beyond the wall of trees, he stumbled on a road. No cars, but it was better than nothing. He veered right and listened for sounds of life. Anything.

Instead, he got more howling wind, which seemed to be picking up steam with each blow. Coconut trees were already twisting in every direction.

If anything happened to Lauren before he got back, he'd never be able to live with himself. The thought of her exposed out on that beach gnawed at his insides. He told himself professional pride had him desperate to see her again, but it was so much more.

Next to the wall of palms, he caught sight of a dark silhouette. Whatever it was, it was substantial. He got close enough to make out the outline of a horse.

It was obvious the horse had been abandoned, left to its own devices. What that said in the bigger sense frustrated him to hell and back, but worked to his advantage for now. He got close enough to make out a saddle on the horse's back.

There were others. They must've been abandoned when the storm intensified. Their bowed backs meant they were old rentals. Trail horses on the island were ridden pretty hard, not coming near the standard of care animals received in the States. They wouldn't scare easily.

Still, they were loose. This would require caution. He located a shed where he found saddles and tack. Jaden slowed his pace as the horse's nostrils flared, spooked.

"You're all right." Jaden used as calm a voice as he could, considering he practically had to shout to cut through the howling wind.

The horse didn't shy away, allowing him to inch closer. That was good.

Moving steadily, Jaden focused on making deliberate actions. He lowered his hand, careful not to lift it too high and give the impression he was a threat.

The knotted ropes hung freely on the ground. When they were inches from his hand the horse snorted, and then took a couple steps backward.

Jaden inched forward again. "Good boy."

The sorrel horse reared its head and turned up its ears, keeping a close eye on Jaden's hand. He took another step, his hand so close it could touch the ropes. The animal bobbed its head before lowering it.

Jaden brought his other hand around and patted

its neck. A crack slammed his right shoulder. Something that felt the size of a softball had nailed him.

Blinding pain followed.

Not wanting the horses to scatter, he swallowed the urge to unleash a torrent of curse words. He glanced down at what had hit him. Coconut. If it had fallen a little bit farther left, he'd be dead.

Jaden edged around the horse while patting its neck.

"Easy."

Moving his hands slowly and steadily, he saddled and bridled the horse. Mounting him, Jaden patted his sloping back. He eased onto the worn saddle that fit like aged leather shoes. Allowing plenty of slack in the reins, He kicked stirrups out of the way and wrapped his feet around the horse's underbelly before giving a slight squeeze. The horse responded, breaking into a trot.

A metal garbage can spun around in front of him, turned, and flew past, not more than a foot from his head. He ducked other flying debris as a two-by-four slammed into a nearby tree. The horse spooked.

"Whoa, boy."

That Jaden desperately needed to get back to Lauren sat heavy in his thoughts. A little voice inside his head said she was more to him than an asset... much more. He dismissed the thought. He was cursed. Everyone Jaden cared about in his personal life died. This was work. She was his mission. He'd promised to help her. He would find a way to uphold his vow.

But how far had he gone down the road? How long could she hold on? Would she still be breathing when he found her again?

CHAPTER 8

THE IMAGE of Lauren curled up, helpless on the beach flashed through Jaden's mind, causing him to rally. He focused, ventured a guess and guided the horse to make a left at a sign for Daybreak Beach.

Once on the sand, he slowed the horse to a walk and scanned the shoreline. Visibility was low. Sand was everywhere—in his eyes, hair, inside his mouth.

"Lauren." The word bounced back in his face.

The wind was thick. His throat cracked from desert-like dryness.

He swung his right leg behind him and slid down the side of the horse. Wrapping the reins around his wrist, he nearly dragged the hefty animal toward the water.

A lump on the sand caught his attention. Could be debris. He moved closer.

Lauren lay half buried in sand.

Not allowing himself a moment to stress, he moved to her side and dropped down on all fours. Relief was a flood to dry planes when she blinked her eyes open.

"Where'd—"

"I'm here," he said soothingly. He didn't want her to waste valuable energy trying to talk.

She managed a slight nod. "I'm okay. Just. Need. Rest."

Winds gusted, nearly knocking Jaden over. The horse shuffled its feet, flared its nostrils, and then shifted around so his hindquarters faced the wind.

"We have to go. Now. I'm going to pick you up."

Lightning bounced off the water. Not a second later, thunder cracked. The horse broke into a full run. With his hand trapped, Jaden tightened his grip, resolved to being dragged across the beach. He brought his left hand up and tried to free his right.

The reins were tangled and wrapped too tightly, cutting off the blood flow through his wrist as he was hauled across the unforgiving sand.

If the horse didn't slow down Jaden would surely be killed once they hit the road.

Where would that leave Lauren? Why was her welfare his first concern when faced with his own mortality?

As the horse crossed the wall of palm trees, for some unknown reason, the animal stopped. Jaden didn't question the stroke of luck as he pulled to his feet with a grunt. He tied the reins to a tree, deciding it'd be safer to bring Lauren to the horse.

Pain rifled through him when he moved. He tried to lift his arm over his head but couldn't move it more than a few inches. His shoulder must have been pulled out of socket. No time to pop it back in. He rubbed his sore spot as he sprinted back toward Lauren.

She was already on her feet struggling against the wind, trying to move away from the sea. Right now she couldn't afford to expend any more energy. Her body had been pushed to the brink as it was.

"Thank God you're all right," she said, her golden eyes wide.

"You're still weak, sweetheart." He scooped her off her feet. He bit down the pain and ran toward the animal. He put her down a few moments later beside the horse and then helped her into the saddle using his good arm. "Ever ride before?"

"No."

Jaden secured the reins, and then jumped onto the horse's back behind Lauren. He wrapped his good arm around her waist and squeezed his heels.

They weren't far from food. Shelter. If his calculations were correct, they were on the east side of the island. A safe house was close by. Gregory should be waiting. There, she would find a place to rest and he could regroup.

Navigating down the road, careful to avoid flying

debris, Jaden was sure they'd come across someone along the way, but there was no one. The storm had everyone battening down the hatches.

Or worse, evacuating.

The gnawing ache in his shoulder threatened to blind him, but at least the pain kept him feeling. He was alive.

And his heart was awakened.

THE WINDS PICKED up speed again, forcing pelting rain and sand into Lauren's face. The combination blistered the skin on her cheeks. Tears began to fall, mixed with the salty taste of rain, before finding their way to chapped, stinging lips. Hope blew away with Mother Nature's pounding fury. Every part of her body ached worse than if she'd been dropped a hundred feet into a wall of water.

She was soaked and hungry. Jaden's thick, muscled arms encircled her waist, pulling her back flat against his chest. His warmth blanketed her shivering frame.

Lauren hadn't needed anyone since her childhood when Max was there for her. Needing Jaden was a foreign feeling at best. Could she trust it?

The sight of a large building snapped her mind to the present.

"Look there. Do you see it?" Was it real or a figment of her delusional mind? She couldn't be sure.

Jaden's arms tightened around her waist. "Hold on."

The horse galloped faster as a building came into focus. Beachside condos. Good. There'd be people. Warmth. Shelter. Food. Water. Help.

Lauren felt herself fading, wanting to crumple over from exhaustion after all that swimming. Jaden guided the horse to the nearest door, jumped down, and tied off the reins to a sign that read: Seascape.

"This is a temporary safe house. I need to make sure it'll be safe. Wait here," he barked. A beat later, he banged on the door.

No one answered, and she had no plans to hang around out there like a sitting duck in a tidal wave.

Lauren dismounted. Her legs gave out, and she landed hard on the pavement. She scrambled to her feet as Jaden rounded the corner where the building faced the sea and a wall of windows would be the standard issue to take advantage of the endless water views.

Lauren ran to the second door and banged. The sound bounced around her, unable to cut through the harsh wind. Her arms burned. It was taking over all of her strength to go this far.

"Help!" She pounded on the door, repeating the word, and then twisted the knob.

The door was locked, and there was no sound except for the howling wind. Come on. Somebody.

Turning to scan the small parking lot, it took only a second to register there were no cars. That sent a lead fireball swirling down her throat. Maybe Jaden was having better luck on the other side.

Gale force-like slammed her back a step as she rounded the corner.

Shimmying onto a balcony, she tried the first slider. Nothing. She pressed her face to the glass. Easy enough to see right through the living room and kitchenette straight to the back door. Typical island getaway.

No Jaden. Or anyone else for that matter.

Lights were on. Cabinets were open. It looked as if the place had been left in a hurry.

That couldn't be good.

Moving onto the next balcony, she pressed her face against the glass. Being met with a similar scene caused her stomach to drop.

This time, the slider opened when she tried it.

"Jaden?"

She ran through checking each room, slamming doors in her path.

The wind howled as it shook the windows. Violent seas outside raged against anything in their path. It was getting harder and harder to move her legs.

The back door blasted open. Lauren jumped. Jaden. Thank God.

"I went outside to check on you. I thought I told you to stay put." His angry voice cracked. His face, red and chaffed, was lined with worry and fatigue.

Stay put?

"I'm a little tired of being told what to do." She stomped past him, but was halted quickly by the strong hand on her arm.

"Look, I wasn't saying—"

"What?" she snapped. "First you rescue me, and then you accuse me of being one of them. Now you want to tell me where to stand and what to do?"

"All I was trying to do was secure the area," he said with his hands in the surrender position.

It wasn't fair to take out all her frustration on him. She owed him. "Sorry. My life was normal yesterday and suddenly I'm being chased by horrible men. In a hurricane. While dodging bullets. I'm not used to dealing with this. My world is simple, uncomplicated. I own my own shop, which was doing pretty well until I mortgaged the hell out of it to save my brother, who will most likely die anyway."

Jaden's lips clamped shut. Exhaustion deepened the lines around his eyes. "You've been brave today. For what it's worth, I'm proud of you."

Now she really felt bad for snapping at him. "Thanks," was all she could manage to say.

"We're set up next door. We'll be safe for now."

She followed him to the condo.

A man who looked to be in his early twenties was there, setting up a machine the size of a small dishwasher.

"This is Gregory," Jaden said.

Lauren introduced herself. She pointed to the hunk of metal in the middle of the dining room. "What is that?"

"A generator," Gregory said. "This place belongs to my cousin. It's not ideal, but it's all we have to work with right now. If this storm gets as bad as they say we could lose power."

A radio squawked and beeped with weather warnings.

Jaden moved to the kitchen where he dug around until he found a large salad bowl. He filled it with water, and then fought the winds outside to bring it to the horse.

After removing the bridle, Jaden held up the bowl for him to drink. Lauren followed, but didn't say anything as she smoothed her hand down the sorrel's neck.

Then Jaden smacked his hindquarters, shooing him away.

Jaden pulled Lauren safely back inside. Looking like almost all the strength had drained out of him, he moved to the kitchen. "We'll be okay here for a while," he said.

Exhaustion was wearing Lauren's nerves thin.

Lightheaded and hungry, she moved to the couch and crumbled onto it.

"I don't think I've ever been this tired before," she said, wanting clean clothes and a shower, but too tired to make a move for either.

Filling a glass with tap water, Jaden quickly drained the contents before refilling it.

A few moments later, he was by her side, looking strained, tired. His face was red from windburn. "Can you sit up?" he asked.

She was up enough to notice his expression that said he might explode from pain movement caused him. Not that he'd admit it. She doubted he'd let anyone get close enough to see anything beyond the external. His face was a study in fortitude. His expression gave away nothing of what he truly thought. He was a professional. A soldier. This was his job.

He held out his palm with two tablets on it. "Pain reliever. This should help."

Lauren propped herself up on one elbow, then tossed the pills in her mouth.

"Your lips are purple. You're cold." He disappeared, returning a moment later with a blanket. "Get out of that wetsuit."

He turned his back, which gave her privacy. "Better?"

"Much. Thanks. That goes for everything you've done for me today. I wouldn't be alive if not for you.

God only knows where I would've ended up." A shudder ran through her.

Lauren's eyelids were heavy weights, adrenaline having faded from her body, and with it, her ability to fight exhaustion. A yawn rolled up and out.

They'd made it to shelter. She had water for a burning tongue and lip balm for dry lips.

Jaden said they'd be safe. No reason to doubt him.

"You hear from Gunner's crew?" Jaden shouted toward the empty hall.

"Not since this morning," Gregory responded.

"They didn't show at the beach."

Gregory reappeared, holding a gun and a cell phone out to Jaden. "This storm has been upgraded, sir. As of now, we should be safe. Might get orders to evacuate though."

Jaden took the weapon and phone, nodding his acknowledgement. "How long?"

"Spotters think we have an hour, maybe more before the big stuff hits. Cell coverage is unreliable. A tower is most likely down."

"Who knows we're here?" Jaden asked.

"Other than headquarters? No one. I called in your location while you were outside. I'm waiting for clearance or extraction orders."

"We were ambushed at the beach. Bryce..." He cast his eyes down.

"Any idea who's responsible?" Gregory's eyes shifted from Lauren to Jaden.

Jaden rolled his shoulders. "The guys I saw looked like they were with Menendez. Get the word out and let's see if we put a stop to their money laundering. Who'd you give my location to?"

"Cynthia." She was a handler.

"Any chance someone else overheard?" Jaden asked. "I have another agent down and I'm tired of casualties."

"Damn," Gregory said with an apologetic look toward Lauren for swearing. "It's getting harder to know who to trust."

CHAPTER 9

A LOUD CRACK shocked Jaden awake. He rubbed his eyes, trying to orient himself. The condo. He'd fallen asleep? He needed to get his bearings.

Gregory had said he called in their arrival. That meant headquarters and anyone else monitoring the networks knew. Since the cartel had pinned his location on the boat, they might have been able to tap into other communications. The storm would slow them down.

An unsettled feeling crept over him. How long had he been out?

His watch said not more than twenty minutes. Still. It wasn't like Jaden to let his guard down while guarding an asset. No matter that protecting Lauren felt completely different from any other mission he'd been on. The others had been work. This was personal. There was something warm and comforting about her that chiseled away at the casing around his heart.

He mentally slapped himself. Distraction could get them both killed.

They were safe for now. He tried to reach Gunner again. Nothing. Wasn't like him to go off the grid like that. Damn. Jaden hoped like hell his boss was all right.

His body ached, but not as much as before.

Lauren was snuggled up to him, her face against his chest. There was a slight pout to her lips, and his body instantly reacted to her. He was growing hard nestled this close.

This was not the time for rogue hormones.

Besides, he'd had enough rest to think clearly. His second though? Bryce. The third operative to be killed in a month.

At first blush, Jaden had figured the situation blew up back at the beach because he'd been spotted. If that were true, shouldn't Jaden be dead and not his buddy? Unless Bryce accidently stepped in the way of a bullet marked for Jaden. Guilt knifed his chest. If Bryce was killed because of Jaden's actions, he'd never forgive himself. He shook his head. Stick to the facts.

Lauren had brought serious cash to the beach. The cartel had shown up ready and armed to stage war. Brought serious metal, AR-15s, and enough ammo to wipe out a small island. Why?

Sure, his agency had been putting quite a bit of heat on the cartels recently. His mind snapped to Camila and her deception that had cost ManTech lives. Max might lead Jaden to her and he could deal with her once and for all.

No one else was going to die on his watch. Keeping Lauren safe until this ordeal was over became his number one priority. He told himself that was the only reason he cared and not because she stirred feelings inside he didn't want to acknowledge. Couldn't acknowledge. If he acknowledged those she'd be dead, too. Jaden had no plans to tempt fate again.

Nursing his sore shoulder, he slipped off the couch and moved to the window as rain pounded the pane. Thunder cracked overhead sounding like it was literally ripping the earth in two. If he were lucky, this would be the worst of the storm, but luck wasn't something experience had taught him to depend on.

He flipped on the kitchen switch. The electricity worked. Light was good. Then again, he could think of a few intriguing ideas involving the woman on the couch and a dark room. He shook off the thought and refocused.

Gregory was set up in the second bedroom monitoring the weather situation.

Crossing to the bathroom, Jaden peeled off both his wetsuit and jockeys. His new cell rang. He answered it, hoping like hell it was Gunner.

"What's the plan?" Her voice was undeniable.

"Helena, I told you we've got this. I have Gregory right here if I need backup." She must've leaned on all her contacts to get his number. She was smart. How the hell was he going to keep her out of this fight? Jaden had no idea if the men who'd killed Smith or Bryce had anything to do with Tim's death.

"You already know how I feel about letting others fight my battles," she said.

He didn't like the sound in her voice. He wished he'd been able to see her, check on her for himself after the funeral. She had every right to be upset. He hadn't been there for her in the way he should. He'd been shot and agency protocol required he be tucked away. He hated the way it felt like he'd turned his back on her when she needed his support most. Support? He stifled a laugh. Helena would see support as charity. She accepted charity from no one. "You heard from Gunner?"

"No."

He paused. "We'll get the guy who killed Tim."

"No, I will." The resignation in her voice said she'd die trying.

"How'd you con someone into giving you this number?" he asked.

"I didn't."

Click.

She must've hacked into the system and started calling random cell numbers until she located him.

She was determined, and he couldn't blame her. On a primal level, he totally understood her need for revenge.

He checked his wounds. They amounted to a handful of scrapes and bruises, except for the golf ball sitting on top of his shoulder from the dislocation. He rotated his arm outward slowly and steadily. He gripped the sink basin. With a grunt, he pushed up on his feet until his muscles and tendons stretched enough for the joint to slide into his shoulder socket.

Relief came instantly. He moved to the shower. The warm water eased his weather-torn body. Closing his eyes, he let the heat penetrate his sore muscles.

Bryce. Someone from the agency would have to tell his girlfriend. Thinking about him tightened the muscles in Jaden's back and neck. His fists clenched.

If he could get Lauren and himself to the primary checkpoint safely, sophisticated communication equipment would be there. He could guarantee her safety. But when? How? The weather sure as hell wasn't cooperating.

This condo was far better than being somewhere out there dodging bullets. He could protect Lauren here. An image of the two of them, swimsuit clad, vacationing at the condo popped into his mind. And kids.

Losing his friends played tricks with his psyche. Jaden shook water out of his hair. Not once had he considered having children. His job was his life, and he was a damn good soldier. And yet, hadn't he been feeling like something was missing lately?

A minute later, he toweled off, wiping the thought from his brain. A toothbrush and toothpaste were heaven about now. Lip balm was next.

"What do you have for us to wear?" he asked, poking his head into Gregory's room.

"In the room. On the bed. I laid out clothes for both of you."

"What's the weather doing?" Jaden asked.

"Stable for now. We're cut off out here from the worst of it. But if this monster turns, we're in bad shape." Gregory twisted his face in a look of concern.

"Still no word from Gunner?"

Gregory shook his head.

"Keep trying to locate him. Use whatever means necessary." He'd tell him to put a trace on Helena's cell if it wouldn't create a backdoor a smart hacker could breach. He needed to keep a closer eye on her. Her blind fury could cause her to rush into a situation when patience was called for. It could cost her life.

Jaden found a white t-shirt, a pair of jeans, and fresh boxers laid out on the bed in the master. There were dry socks and tennis shoes, too. His version of Christmas morning.

He slipped them on.

They only clothes he found on the other side of

the bed were horrible, sack-looking dresses. He stifled a laugh. He seriously doubted he could force one of those on Lauren. She'd look hot in anything she put on, but she wouldn't think so.

Suddenly, the image of her standing in the boat wearing nothing but a white lace bra and panties flashed in his brain. His earlier erection tried to revive itself. Traitor.

Lauren awakened his emotions. Brought a glimpse of light into the darkest corners of his heart. He cancelled the thought, reminding himself that she was an asset.

Jaden seriously needed to control his hormones.

He shuffled through drawers until he found something suitable for her. A pair of jeans and t-shirt.

Sizing them up, he grinned. She'd fit.

After folding the outfit and placing it on a chair in the living room, he dug around in the kitchen. They needed food. He was hungry, tired and beaten. His shoulder still ached. All in all, a hell of a lot better than he'd been half an hour ago.

Surprisingly, none of it mattered. Jaden felt alive being back in the field. Even though the woman sleeping in the next room played tricks on his emotions. He couldn't ignore the simple fact that she picked at the chinks in his armor. She threatened to bring parts of him back to the light that had long since been buried...and were better left dormant.

Lauren stirred. He glanced over and then moved to her side. He took a knee.

She was so close his fingers tensed from wanting to go rogue and trail the curves of her back, get lost in that fiery mane. He swallowed hard as he strained painfully inside his shorts. The traitor was back.

"Wake up, sweetheart. Not sure how much longer we'll be able to stick around here." He wanted her to eat.

She looked groggy and small as she sat up. He smiled. Small was the furthest word from his mind when it came to describing her personality.

"Has to be safer than out there, right?" she asked through a sleepy yawn.

She stretched those long, lean runners legs, looking sexy as hell.

A sudden urge to kiss the small freckle above her lip overcame him. *Not the time, soldier.* Pointing to clothes neatly stacked on a side chair, he said, "Wasn't sure about your size. Looks like they'll fit."

Her focus bounced from the pile of clothes back to meet his. Hurt darkened her eyes. "They'll be fine. At least they're dry."

Jaden rest an elbow on his knee. He didn't blame her for looking at him like that. Especially when they were back on the rocks and he'd all but accused her of working with the cartel. The pain of his accusation had sizzled in her eyes ever since.

Regret formed a lump in his throat. Why was it

easier to push her away than to face the rogue feelings inside him?

He stood and moved into the kitchen, filling a plate for her.

"Eat something." He walked to her and handed over the items.

"Those windows don't look safe," she said taking a bite of the roll as if it were a steak dinner. "Think they'll hold?"

"I honestly don't know."

"Guess we'll figure it out soon enough," she said.

Her gaze appraised him suspiciously. He didn't like it. But he couldn't deny he deserved it. If he'd trusted her, he would've told her the truth already about her brother.

Gaining her trust was mission-critical but he couldn't bring himself to trick her into talking. He'd had no problem using whatever means at his disposal to turn an asset before. So why all of a sudden was he developing a conscience?

"I was honest with you before," he said. "I really don't know who ultimately hired me. I don't always know."

"Then how can you be sure you're working for one of the good guys?" she asked after taking a sip of the water her brought over for her.

"That much I can tell you. We take assignments from the government and large corporations. We bring down cartels, terrorists, governments, and bad guys."

She repositioned herself, sitting a bit straighter against the couch as she stopped chewing.

"Criminals like my brother?"

"Yes. Like Max. And a lot of other types of evil."

She dropped the roll, didn't speak.

"I'm sorry. You might be related, but he's one of them," he said.

"I know. Believe me, I know. I hate what he's become. I do. It's just hard to hear. I've turned my back on it for so long now. Pretended it wasn't happening. And look where that got me." She glanced around, wincing when thunder clapped loudly. "I'd still rather not know, to be honest."

"Look. There's something else I need to tell you about Max."

CHAPTER 10

Lauren sat up, rigid, her back ramrod straight now, her brown-gold eyes wide. "Which is?"

"He was planning to testify against a dangerous criminal group." Why did he feel the need to tell her this? He'd always played his hand close to his chest.

A look of pure disbelief darkened her features. "And you didn't tell me that before?"

"I had to know that I could trust you first." Her reaction couldn't have hurt more than a knife to Jaden's heart. "Which bothers me because it makes even less sense why they kidnapped him."

He resisted the urge to wrap her in his arms and take her confusion away. She'd probably fight back. And he deserved it. He momentarily forgot she was part of a case again, which wasn't like him at all. He'd never compromised an assignment by getting emotional with an asset.

"Can you actually get away from bad men like these?"

He nodded. "It's rare though and not without consequences."

Lauren set the plate down beside her and got to her feet quickly. She paced as thunder rolled in the distance. "He called a couple of times recent. I ignored him. I should've—"

"Look. Don't do this. I didn't tell you before because I didn't want you to blame yourself."

"We both know you didn't tell me because you didn't trust me. Even so, I had a right to know," she said, her eyes practically shooting daggers at him.

Jaden didn't speak. A slip of conscience niggled at him. She was right on both counts.

"Then why? Why did they take him?"

"That's the game-show-winning question. It wasn't to kill him. They would have done that already."

Her pace quickened, and she chewed on her thumbnail. "Is it because of the money? They wanted more. Maybe he owed them or had to buy his way out?"

These guys didn't usually kidnap for cash owed. Ordinarily, they chopped men up and buried the pieces deep in a South American jungle. That information he would keep to himself. "Not their usual style of collection."

"So there's more to it."

"Which could be tied to my agency," he admitted.

"When they called, they put him on the phone. He begged me not to come. Said they'd just kill me too." Large round droplets were spilling from her eyes now. "He sounded resigned to dying and thought I would, too."

"That couldn't have been easy to hear." Damn. She'd been through enough already and here Jaden was piling on more. He didn't like being the one to tell her this. He wanted to be her protector, blocking out everything bad or threatening. He told himself she'd think more clearly without distractions and not because he was developing feelings for her. The kiss on the rocky island had imprinted him. He could still taste her sweet lips.

Find her brother and they'd have answers. Jaden was almost certain that one of Menendez's boys had killed Tim. Camila was responsible for Smith's death.

A gust of wind slammed the windows.

Lauren gasped.

Jaden popped to his feet. "Better grab a shower while we still have hot water. I have no idea if the generator will hold. Toothbrush is on the counter. Found some new ones in the cabinet. Everything you need is in there."

Nodding, she grabbed the clothes stack and darted toward the bathroom.

Jaden waited outside the door, debating his next move. Their safe house was an old military compound. The condo, being a makeshift location, was therefore more vulnerable. The storm tripled the threat. Also made it more difficult to leave.

The lights dimmed, and then Jaden found himself standing inside a black hallway.

Lauren screamed.

Jaden opened the door so fast it smacked against the wall.

"What is it?"

"C-c-cold."

The faucet turned off and a few moments later Lauren appeared wrapped in a towel. Lightning lit up the small hallway. She stood there shivering.

"How about that generator?" Jaden shouted to Gregory.

"Sorry. I'm working on it. For now, power's gone," Gregory called from the other room.

Jaden retrieved another towel and moved to her. It took all his energy to cover her with the cloth and look away from the soft curve of her bare shoulder, which glistened with tiny beads of water.

"You ever been through anything like this before?" Lauren asked as Jaden led her into the living room.

The volume rose on the radio in the other room, cutting through the winds.

"Trust me. We'll get through this. You know that, right?" He lowered his voice.

She didn't respond or budge. Panic must've caused her to freeze. Losing self-control wasn't good.

She'd been through a lot already. If she slipped into shock…game over.

Jaden took her in his arms to warm her. Pulling her close did little else but cause her lilac scent to fill his senses. "I won't let anything happen to you."

Her long lashes swept up, and her golden eyes stared into his. "I know," she said softly.

Jaden sighed sharply, unsure of why he felt compelled to offer reassurance, to tell her what he'd never spoken aloud before when all he wanted to do was cover her mouth with his kisses. "Believe me when I say I know how important finding your brother is to you."

She broke eye contact. "You can't possibly know what this is like. Not when you go around saving people all the time."

"That's where you're wrong. I had a brother once, too."

Her gaze came up to meet his. "What happened?"

"He was four years older than me. Got involved in the wrong crowd in high school. Drugs. He was small time. Got shot and killed when a deal went bad." His voice caught. His fists clenched and released. "He was just a kid. Didn't know what he was doing. He died for forty dollars. That's what they took from him as they stepped over him and left him for dead."

She lifted her gaze to study his face, examining every curve, as though his confession explained a lot.

"It's the real reason you do this job, isn't it? Because you couldn't save him."

He shrugged, non-committal. He didn't want to examine his actions any more than he wanted to face the shaft of light to his heart brought on by her smile.

"Why're you telling me this now?"

He rolled his shoulders, winced. Damned if he knew. He wanted, no needed, her to know she was different. "I wanted to be honest. With you. With myself. Show you I'd never fight this hard for the wrong side."

She paused, looking everywhere but at him. Clearing his throat, he tried to break free from the fog clouding his judgment. He should walk away. He should fight the instinct he had to hold her, touch her, and tell her everything she wanted to hear.

Should have. Would have. Could have.

But didn't.

So he kissed her.

SANITY MUST'VE TAKEN over a few seconds after their lips touched because Jaden pulled back. But for a moment, Lauren got lost. Lost in the strong and dangerous man's arms. Lost in the fleeting feeling of comfort he provided. Lost in the hope that this whole situation would magically work out.

The silence between them reassured Lauren. It

shouldn't. She reminded herself she should be angry and hurt that he'd held back information after everything they'd been through together.

Then she really saw the hollow cast to his eyes. The dark circles. The story that lurked just beyond those cool baby blues. The pain. He'd opened up to her a little. For a man used to being alone, it must've taken a lot.

Just then, he leaned in so close that his lips grazed her hair, and he whispered, "I believe in you."

His soft words and warm breath on her neck made her lightheaded. She took in a steadying breath, fearing that if he got any closer the gravitational orbit that surrounded him would take over, pulling her into his solid-wall chest where she'd melt.

A crush of emotions knotted in Lauren's stomach, climbed, and lodged in her chest. Her throat tightened, making it impossible to swallow. Quietness blanketed the room as deafening as the roaring winds had been. She could hear Jaden's heart beating steadily, securely inside his chest. The rhythm comforted her.

The winds outside calmed as though Mother Nature had a remote control and had hit pause.

"We need to make our move soon," he said.

With her index finger, Lauren outlined the muscles in Jaden's forearm—his thick, ripped arms.

How sexy was he?

Her head was spinning, her body tingling. He was

perfection. And she had to fight every instinct she had to wrap her arms around his strong neck and beg him to kiss her again. The thought of their last kiss made her lips tingle, wanting more. "Do we have a few minutes to come up with a plan before making our next move?"

Jaden's finger traced her lips before moving to outline her jawbone, his every touch flaming her insides, sending volts of desire through her. She wanted to let go, to trust it would all work out, but her childhood hadn't been spent dreaming of white towers, horses, and handsome dark knights. Hers had been spent protecting herself from nearly everyone.

She refocused her attention on Jaden's face. Taking in all the pain behind those dark eyes, she asked, "You said you had a brother. Is there any other family back home?"

"No."

"Surely there's someone you need to get back to," she said.

"If you're talking about women, there've been a few."

Next time she felt the urge to ask a question she didn't want the answer to, she'd try to remember to keep her mouth shut. She had a past. He had a past. Did they really need to know every detail?

"This job doesn't exactly lend itself to long-term relationships. Not when I'm gone with assignment eleven months out of the year. Not a lot of women are willing to put up with that," he said with his dry crack of a smile.

She figured plenty wouldn't mind waiting for a man as sexy as Jaden. She couldn't help but wonder how many women had trailed behind him trying to get him to leave his job and commit. A few? A couple dozen?

One look at him said the number had to be high. She had eyes. The man was drop dead gorgeous, dark and mysterious. A potent combination that would drive most women into frenzy.

Out of the corner of his mouth he said, "There've been a lot of women. But no one special."

Not sure if she dreamed he'd said it or if she'd even heard him correctly. It didn't matter. She wanted nothing more than to feel his warm skin against hers.

The man in front of her was real. Made her body flame with passion. Desire made every nerve ending from the crown of her head to the tips of her toes tingle with anticipation, need. A distant little voice reminded her how truly dangerous a man like him was.

When his erection pressed against her, all rational thought flew out the window. She'd wanted this man from the moment she saw him. He brought her entire body to life, and she didn't know how much longer she could hold back.

They were face-to-face. Body to body. Skin to

skin. She had nothing more than a towel wrapped around her.

JADEN WASN'T THINKING CLEARLY, couldn't formulate a coherent argument as to why the moment between him and Lauren shouldn't happen. It had all the earmarks of disaster written all over it, but he was too involved to care. Being with her made him wish for things he shouldn't.

So he defied logic and pulled her closer, moving to the back bedroom to ensure a moment of privacy.

"And Lauren. I'm not like those men from your past. You don't have to be afraid of me." He set his jaw, wanting her to hear those words and take them to heart. "I'll take care of you if you let me."

She looked up at him with wide golden eyes, glittery with desire, before squeezing them shut and burrowing into his chest. Before he could say or do anything he found himself holding onto the shaking beauty. Lauren. She was right there in his arms where he wanted her. And it felt so right.

"I believe you," she said.

He stroked her hair as he leaned forward until his lips were within an inch of the nape of her neck. His heart thumped against his rib cage.

The pain rifling his body a distant memory, replaced by an ache to feel her bare skin against his.

To wrap her in his arms and feel her long legs alongside his.

A thin piece of cotton couldn't insulate the raw sexual heat between them.

Her body quaked under his touch, while something deep within him needed to make her feel wanted and safe. His breath thickened. He couldn't think straight. She felt so right in his arms, fit him perfectly.

"Do you trust me?" he asked, and it was important for him to know the answer. She'd already told him she spent way too much of her childhood fearing men. He needed her to believe he wasn't like them.

"Yes," she said.

Sure, she was flawless. Big brown-gold eyes. Taut body. That wasn't what made the image of her replay in his mind relentlessly like a hit song on the radio. It wasn't the soft curve of her hip, endless legs, the way her full, luscious lips fell into a pout. It was the strength and courage she displayed in the face of danger. And something more, something deeper that he didn't want to examine further.

Jaden trailed his finger along the tender part of her arm. Should he even be touching a woman who was tightly linked to his case? An asset?

Consequences be damned.

He couldn't stop if he tried.

The way she reacted to his lightest touch, her

body quaking under his fingertips, made him want more.

Without another word, Jaden pressed a kiss to the small freckle above her lip before his lips found hers, pressing down hungry and needy. Her mouth moved against his, her tongue teasing his.

The creak of the slider opening in the next room scarcely registered over the sounds of the rain and the thundering of his own heart.

Agency guys wouldn't sneak in.

This wasn't good. Their position had been compromised. How in the hell had that happened?

The obvious answer was that someone in his agency couldn't be trusted.

He eased back to look Lauren square in the eyes as he pressed his index finger to his lips.

In barely a whisper, he said, "I haven't stopped thinking about you since the boat. So, believe me, we're going to finish this later."

The reality only headquarters and Gregory knew his location weighed heavily on his thoughts. *And Helena*, he corrected.

Her call might've put him in jeopardy.

Her phone could be hacked.

Damn.

That was exactly why he didn't want her anywhere near this case.

"Someone's here," he whispered to Lauren.

CHAPTER 11

LAUREN FUMBLED for her jeans and t-shirt, her heart racing as Jaden disappeared down the hall. She located a bra, which was a little too small but would do, quickly dressed, and crouched low on the side of the bed.

Tension braided her nerves. Jaden had already proven he was more than competent at his job, but if something happened to him she'd be alone with whomever or whatever lurked on the other side of that wall.

Had she really become dependent on him this quickly? Granted, he had saved her life more times than she could count in the short time she'd known him. Even so, it wouldn't do any good to get too comfortable in the feeling Jaden would always be there to save her.

He was a professional. This was his job. As soon as this was over, he'd be gone.

Where would that leave her? Heartbroken? The admission startled her. She was allowing herself to get carried away with a man she shouldn't trust.

Besides, if anything happened to her where would that leave Max?

"We have to move. *Now*." His tone was hushed but clear as he rounded the side of bed.

A wave of relief washed over her at seeing him again.

"I heard noises," she said, swallowing hard. "Is it the guys from the beach?"

His hand closed on hers protectively as he led her into the bathroom where they both slipped behind the door.

She clamped down the urge to ask about Gregory. Was he out there, too?

The voices in the next room might be low, but they could have been standing over Lauren shouting for the effect they had. Her stomach free-fell to her toes when she heard those terse South American accents. There were at least two. One was familiar. She recognized it from the phone call the other day.

Another one of them was getting closer.

Jaden held up a steadying hand meant to calm her.

In his other hand, metal glinted. She couldn't make it out, but prayed it was something useful, like his gun.

The sound of wet shoe clamping against the white tile floor echoed down the hall.

Other than that, everything was quiet.

Eerily quiet.

Lauren feared her heart beat so loudly those jerks would hear it and she and Jaden would be caught.

An intruder poked his head into the bathroom.

In a sweeping fluid motion, Jaden pulled the guy inside and knocked him unconscious with a powerful jab. Whatever he had in his hand was blunt enough to knock a grown man out cold.

Lauren gasped despite herself.

As Jaden dragged him into the tub, Lauren saw he wore jeans, tennis shoes, and a white shirt. Jaden pulled out his cell, snapped a pic of the guy's face, and hit Send. Before she could blink, his phone was back in his pocket, and his attention was on the door.

Quick footsteps pressed the tile. The second prowler must've heard her.

Jaden slid behind the shower curtain as assailant number two rounded the corner and faced Lauren.

He was tall and muscular. She had to look up to see his face. Lightning flashed. Black, beady eyes stared at her. His wicked half grin said he didn't mind them being alone. An icy chill ran down her spine.

The floral shower curtain must've shielded his buddy and Jaden from view. Beady Eyes holstered his gun and made a move toward Lauren.

The power surged, and lights blinked on.

Beady Eyes' expression tensed as Jaden appeared from behind the curtain, gun drawn and pointed directly at a spot on the Latino's forehead. His facial expression changed from triumph to panic. His pupils dilated from fear. His hands came up in surrender. "I'm not here to make trouble."

"Too late for that," Jaden said.

Lauren fought the urge to panic. "I recognize his voice. He's one of the men who hurt my brother," she said, still stunned, her own voice thin and scared. "It's him."

"You better start talking faster than a preacher on collection plate Sunday," Jaden said.

"I won't tell you jack shit," the man said.

Jaden's finger twitched on the trigger mechanism. "You want to do this the hard way? Fine. Hands against the wall."

Beady Eyes hesitated.

"If you think you can pull that gun from your holster before I can squeeze this trigger, go for it." Jaden's tone left no room for doubt.

A look of resignation crossed his features. He placed his hands against the wall.

Lauren took a step back into the tub and plastered her back against the wall, hoping it would hold her upright. The palpable smell of blood made her knees weak. Her stomach dry-heaved. "Where's Gregory?"

Jaden shook his head.

"Get a gun," he said to Lauren, cocking his head toward the crumpled guy at her feet.

Her heartbeat kicked up another notch, pounding painfully in her chest. She had no idea what to do with a weapon. Her gaze shifted from Beady Eyes to the man at her feet. Jaden needed her help. Never mind that she was fighting the urge to faint. These men hurt Max, and would kill her if they had the chance. She held her breath, bent over, and fumbled around for a weapon.

"Good job," Jaden said to Lauren as she palmed a gun with a shaky hand and pointed it at Beady Eyes.

"If he so much as flinches, shoot."

Could she kill a man? Even *this* man? A man who'd beaten her brother? Possibly killed him? Anger rose in her throat burning a hot trail. She said a little prayer it wouldn't come to that.

Jaden disarmed Beady Eyes, and then thrust his arms behind his back.

"Who was responsible for what happened on the beach? Where's Max?" The anger in his voice startled Lauren. Then she remembered his friend was dead. Given Jaden's background, he was most likely showing remarkable restraint.

Beady Eyes turned his head, and then he winced as his face was shoved against the door.

Lauren kept his gun trained on him.

His gaze narrowed as he focused on her. "Chuparla, bitch."

Beady Eyes whirled around, and Jaden slammed his knee into the guy's gut. Before he could react, the Latino ended up flat on his back on the ground in the hallway with Jaden straddling the man's torso. His arms were tight to his side, trapped by Jaden's unyielding thighs.

Jaden's gaze swept the hallway, reminding Lauren other bad guys could be lurking nearby.

She stepped over the unconscious guy in the tub and stood over Beady Eyes. "Where's my brother? What have you done to him?"

He grinned. White crooked teeth contrasted against his dark brown skin.

"You heard the lady. Where's her brother?" Jaden demanded, shoving the barrel of his gun into the guy's forehead hard enough to leave a mark.

Beady Eyes glared at them. "Do you see him here?" He paused a beat. "Me, either."

"Right. You're nothing. Your bosses would never trust you with important information," Jaden taunted.

"Do you think he knows where Max is?" she asked Jaden.

"You sure this is the guy?"

"Yes. I think. I mean I was so freaked out on the phone I can't be sure, but it sounds like him." Hearing his voice again had her shaking with a mix of fear, anger, and resentment.

With one hand, Jaden pulled his cell from his back pocket, snapped a pic, and hit Send. His other held the insurance Beady Eyes wouldn't move to his forehead. "Gotcha."

He pocketed his cell, and then jerked Beady Eyes to his feet, forcing him to walk in front of them. "Move."

Lauren followed closely behind as Jaden led them into the living room. She gasped when she saw Gregory slumped over in the corner. His lifeless eyes were open and a wire wrapped around his neck.

Jaden made quick work of tying Beady Eyes to a chair before moving to Lauren.

"Gregory," she said in almost a whisper.

Jaden's lips thinned and she could see the frustration and grief in his eyes. His presence brought a sense of calm it shouldn't have as his hand closed around her arm reassuringly, moving her out of earshot.

"If this guy doesn't know where my brother is, does that mean Max is...?" She couldn't bring herself to finish the question.

"They most likely transferred Max to another location. The guys heading operations like these don't take chances. They move victims around, using different people each time. I doubt this scumbag would know where the new location is. But he'd know if he handed Max off alive."

Alive? Oh, God. Lauren thought she might be sick.

His attention turned to the screen on his phone. "The first scumbag has been identified. He works for the Menendez cartel out of Venezuela. We know a few of their hiding spots. One of our female agents, Helena, has been working with them for months. She'll know where to look."

"Won't matter if they think they don't need Max, right?" She could barely bring herself to ask.

"I'm sure he's okay," Jaden said. "We haven't figured out the real reason they took him. It wasn't money."

"Sounds like an operation they have down pat," Lauren said, hating the panic in her voice.

"These are the same guys who smuggle little girls out of our country and sell them into the sex trade. When they're not doing that, they're funneling money in. They have sophisticated channels set up like you wouldn't believe."

Lauren's shoulders dropped forward. With effort, she forced her back straight, refusing to let them win. She wouldn't cry anywhere near those jerks. They didn't deserve the satisfaction. "It sounds so hopeless."

"Not hopeless, sweetheart. We'll find him. I can't figure out one thing though. Why are they looking for you? They must want you something awful to come looking in a hurricane."

A shiver ran down Lauren's spine. Why would they want her? She hadn't done anything wrong. She'd never once so much as cheated on her tax return. She drove the speed limit. "They don't know me, except that I'm related to Max. I haven't gotten mixed up with anyone bad that I know of. Work is my life." She searched his face, needing him to believe her. "Is it the money?"

He shrugged. "None of it makes sense. You're not involved. So why keep coming at you?"

"How on earth did they find us here? And Gregory..." Tears streamed down her cheeks.

"He could've been involved. We find Max and we'll get answers to both our questions," Jaden said quickly.

Did something warm flicker in his eyes?

"Don't you mean if he's still alive?" she asked.

"He is," Jaden said confidently.

It was confidence Lauren wished she had, but didn't. Max's situation had never felt more hopeless to her. A hot tear broke loose and raced down her cheek. "How can you be so sure?"

"Professional hunch," he said calmly.

How he was being so cool, she had no clue. The whole situation had her nerves jittery.

One glance in the corner toward Gregory had her stomach churning. "Your instincts always right?"

"I've only been wrong once before," he said.

"Let's hope this doesn't make twice," she said, but he didn't hear. He'd already moved back to the South American.

"Where'd you take the gringo?"

Beady Eyes' lips thinned. He said nothing.

"Oh, you want to do this the hard way? That works too," Jaden said. He palmed a set of matches, lit the first one, and held it against the guy's hairline.

He shook his head, and then huffed out a breath. The flame flickered and extinguished. His black eyes were unreadable.

Jaden lit another match and waved it close to the Latino. "He still alive?"

Beady Eyes nodded.

"Where then?"

"I already said I don't know."

"Fine." Jaden balled up a piece of paper before setting it on fire. He dropped it in the Latino's lap.

CHAPTER 12

BEADY EYES BUCKED, trying to knock the lit match off his lap. "Damn. I told you everything I know. I swear."

"I'm slow. Give me a recap." Jaden stood there.

Lauren's body tensed as she waited for the answers.

"He's alive. I handed him off this morning." His black eyes now wider with panic. "Now get that thing off my lap before you fry my nuts."

"You the one who beat him?"

Beady Eyes squirmed, the heat obviously becoming too much for him. "Hurry up. This ain't cool. Take it off."

"Okay. If you say so. One thing first." Jaden dealt a blow that left the guy unconscious.

He picked up the ball of fire and threw it in the sink. A second later, he stripped the Latin guy's weapons, moved to the patio, and tossed all but one of the guns over the sea wall.

"Insurance," he said to Lauren. Then, he pulled the guy's cell phone from his pocket and tried to unlock it. Jaden closed his fist around the SIM card. "Might be able to get something out of this at headquarters."

He moved to the bathroom next, with Lauren trailing close behind. He stopped long enough to tie the Latino's arms and feet together and snatch his key ring. "That should hold him. Give us time."

Lauren followed him into the kitchen.

"We need supplies. Find whatever you can. A paring knife. Fruit. Water. Anything that might keep us alive in case we don't make it to the safe house." Jaden approached the back door. A gust of wind smacked it against the wall as soon as he opened it. "We need to move. Our location has been compromised. More men are probably on the way already."

Fear gripped Lauren. Her stomach rumbled. There was no way she could eat but her stomach reminded her it had been too long since her last meal.

A voice in her head reminded her that against all odds Jaden had kept her alive.

She sure didn't plan to hang around in the condo alone with a dead man in the living room, an unconscious man in the shower, and his clone close by. She trusted Jaden to get them to safety. He'd made the right calls so far, managing to keep them alive despite their circumstances.

Thunder clapped. Before Lauren could rationalize her thoughts, she found Jaden and burrowed into his chest.

He wrapped strong arms around her and brushed a kiss on her forehead.

She couldn't stop herself from wondering if he felt the same sense of comfort when they were this close as she did, not that it was relevant now. More men with guns waited out there.

In here, they'd been safe for a little while. She wished she could linger in that feeling as long as possible. No more thoughts about her brother. No more thoughts about the raging storm outside. No more feeling empty and alone...

"You okay?" Jaden asked, searching her face, looking at her like he couldn't quite read what was on her mind.

She collected her random thoughts. She hadn't come all this way to stop now. "Fine."

"Let's get out of here and get to safety. Then we'll take care of these." He motioned toward her bumps and bruises.

"Meaning your safe house?" she asked.

Jaden nodded. "Shirley Heights."

"Can we trust it?" Lauren asked, unsure if Jaden could honestly answer yes.

He shrugged. "It's our best chance of survival

right now. We can't stay here. The location's been compromised. We have no choice but to go for it."

Lauren took the hand being held out to her and followed Jaden through the door.

The brush underfoot was thick. Her foot tangled, and she nearly lost her balance. Jaden's hand steadied her. She looked up in time to catch a glimpse of something colorful and substantial. "What's that?"

As they moved closer, she got a good look at the bright yellow beacon. She kept an eye out for falling debris as Jaden guided then to a yellow 4x4.

The Jeep, a soft-top complete with window zippers, wouldn't offer great support but was better than being completely exposed to the elements.

Jaden pressed his face against the plastic window. "The keys are inside."

He secured the supplies behind her chair, scuttled around to the driver's side, and then climbed in.

He wasted no time cranking the engine.

Glory of all glories, it started on the first try.

He tapped the gauges. "Can't be sure about the gas. Says it's full, but these old Jeeps are notorious for floating needles."

"Think we'll be alone at the next safe house?" She had to shout to be heard over the rain and wind lashing the Jeep.

The Wrangler rocked back and forth as Jaden gunned it. He jammed the gearshift while he stomped the gas pedal. "It's top secret. Not even

Gregory knew about it. Even so, I can't be sure until I get there."

He didn't need to say more. She realized pretty quickly all that he meant.

Cranking the wheel left, he just missed a tree branch sailing through the sky. He had to slam the steering wheel right to avoid another that nearly careened into them.

The Jeep was old to begin with, and it was taking a beating. The windows started fogging, and the big crack across the front made it nearly impossible to see out the window.

She looked up in time to see a thicket. A palm tree broken in half and a few other mangled trees completely blocked the road. "Watch out."

Jaden nailed the brake, and they both flew forward. The Jeep spit, sputtered, and fishtailed until it came to a stop at the edge of the rubble.

Seeing the road was completely blocked, he vaulted from the Jeep and went to work quickly clearing debris and untangling branches.

Lauren hopped from the passenger seat in time to yell, "Look out!"

A palm tree spun around in the sky, and then flew straight into Jaden's side, knocking him onto the mound of debris.

"Oh. God. No." By the time she got to him, he was slumped over on top of the heap.

Winds howled as she gingerly turned his face

around. His head moved too easily. If he didn't survive, she'd surely die too.

She felt for a pulse. Got one.

"Jaden."

The branch had probably knocked him unconscious. His forehead was gashed, and the cut was wet with rain and blood.

Lauren couldn't imagine the situation getting any worse. Fear ravaged her. Rain pelted her face, stinging her eyes.

She gently tapped Jaden's cheek with the flat of her hand. "C'mon."

With a severe shake of his head, Jaden sat upright. "I'm all right."

He grinned a haughty, sexy little grin, no doubt meant to abate any doubts about just how fine he felt and then bound to his feet. His gaze locked onto the road behind them. "We gotta get out of here. *Now.*"

The sense of urgency in his voice skyrocketed.

"What is it?" Sure, the weather was an issue but he hinted at something worse. .

"Get in the Jeep and drive," he said.

"What do you mean?" What are you planning to do?"

"Go. And don't look back."

"What about—"

"I'll meet you. Don't worry. I'll stay back and cover you." He wedged behind the mound of debris, pulled out his new gun, and took aim.

Lauren turned in time to see a black SUV speeding toward them.

Her hands shook from adrenaline. Determination welled in her chest. She refused to give up. But leaving Jaden? The one man who'd kept her alive this long?

His plan had better work. Whatever that was. He had better find her again.

She would not survive without him.

Lauren hopped into the driver's seat. She wanted to scream and cry, but what would that accomplish?

Slamming the gearshift into Reverse, adrenaline pulsing through her arms providing a boost of octane-like strength, she practically stripped the gears trying to back up the truck.

The motor coughed, chugged, and then stopped.

She mashed the clutch and stomped on the gas pedal. Next, she jiggled the key.

The Jeep growled.

"C'mon." She cranked they key again after giving the truck a moment to rest. Nothing. She sucked in a breath before trying again. The engine whirred but didn't catch.

Pumping the pedal harder, she prayed she wouldn't flood the engine.

Please. Don't do this...

Suddenly the engine hummed as the Jeep vibrated to life.

"You got this," she said, trying to rally. She stole a

glance toward Jaden for support. He was huddled behind the debris. Tap. Tap. Tap. Flashes of light shot from the barrel of his gun. The SUV had stopped, the doors were splayed open, and men were answering the firestorm.

She slammed the gearshift into Reverse, and then jammed it back into Drive as she nailed the gas.

Inching the truck forward, she wretched the emergency brake when the tires spun. The last thing she needed was for this baby to roll backwards at a critical moment.

Battling worsening weather conditions and her own scattered nerves, Lauren gripped the steering wheel until her knuckles went white. The sounds of gunfire tapped all around her.

Inside the Jeep felt like a time tested tornado shelter compared to what waited on the other side of the thin aluminum door.

She could do this. Just like everything else in life, when pressed, she'd found she could do almost anything. There'd been no choice then and none now. This hunk of metal on four balding tires had to roll over the barrier.

Tires spun as she eased on the gas pedal. She released the emergency brake. The vehicle began its crawl at a frustrating pace. The wipers on the Jeep couldn't clear slobber off a baby's chin, and the head-lights were even less effective. Water and fog combined into a thick wall that decreased visibility next to nothing.

And she hoped like everything there wouldn't be anything else on the road. She was straining to see past the front end of the Jeep as it was. She was thankful, at least, for four-wheel drive.

The Jeep tires ground on top of branches as it continued its climb. Then came a loud thud. Lauren's foot slipped off the gas. The Jeep rolled backward. She mashed the brake.

Lauren wiped fog from the windshield. It streaked. Damn. She couldn't see any better. If anything, she'd just made it worse.

She nailed the gas, but nothing happened. The sound of tires spinning out reverberated in the rain, the whirring noise trapped in the space around her. No forward movement.

Another crush of panic caught in her chest. Something slammed into the back of the Jeep. Had she been hit by a bullet? She scanned her shirt for blood. Relief flooded her when she found none.

Jaden?

CHAPTER 13

PANIC GRIPPED Lauren as she glanced around. No. Thank God, Jaden was fine. She didn't even want to think what she'd do if he was hit.

Pressing the gas pedal harder, the Jeep rocked back and forth. With a loud thump and a chug, the truck broke free, and she navigated it to the top of the hump.

Tap. Tap. Tap.

The sound of rapid gunfire nearly stopped her heart as she crested and then drove as fast as she could until she recognized nothing. Her pulse galloped. She had to remind herself that this was his job. This was what he did for a living.

He'd told her to keep driving, and that's what she intended to do. He would turn up again. A few minutes passed when she saw a dark figure in front her waving his arms. Jaden?

God, she hoped.

If not, she was as good as dead out there with nothing to protect her. She slammed the brake, fishtailing. The figure, head down, came to the passenger side. Lauren's foot shook on the pedal.

Relief fueled her when she got a good look at Jaden's face. "You're alive."

He nodded as he climbed in.

"But how did you get that far ahead of me?" She realized that he must know the area.

"Winding roads," he said, repositioning to take aim out the back of the Jeep.

"What about your forehead? You took a nasty crack before," Lauren said, putting the Jeep in Drive and stomping the gas pedal.

"That explains the headache." His fingers searched his face as if making sure he still had two eyes, a nose, and a mouth. "Just gimme a minute. I can take over when I'm sure we're safe."

"Are you kidding? Not with that gash." Always the strong one who took care of himself and others around him, Lauren figured she and Jaden had more than a few things in common.

"You're doing great driving in this," Jaden said.

Her heart squeezed at the compliment.

He pulled off his shirt, balled it up, and used it to wipe clean the inside of the windshield. Did he catch her eyeing his bare chest? He must've because he cracked a devastating little grin as he shrugged into his shirt. He was all calm confidence while her heart pounded her ribs painfully.

"Are we lost?" she asked after winding along the path for what felt like half an hour.

"No. I think if we make a couple of good turns, we can find the old military barracks," he reassured.

A solid wood door whisked through the air, spun around in front of the Jeep's windshield, and then crashed down on top of the hood. Lauren let out a scream before she could clamp it down. The vehicle stopped.

Grabbing the balled up supplies from the back seat, Jaden shouted, "We better move out."

He rolled out of the seat. Lauren scrambled after him, watching the Jeep disappear over a ledge.

Jaden turned and shouted, "Get down!"

Lauren dropped to her knees, and then fell flat on her stomach. Hugging the ground, mud squishing through her fingers, she followed Jaden as tightly as he could.

Clinging to barren clumps of shrubbery, she clawed her way uphill. Lightning cut across the sky before plunging down with an explosion of thunder.

"There it is," he shouted as he crested the next mound.

Lauren scuttled to his side. A loud crack sounded.

Spinning around, she glimpsed a palm tree as it split in half, unleashing a torrent of coconuts. Jaden dove on top of her, shielding her with his heft. A few slammed him instead. He unleashed a string of swear words.

Before she could utter a thank you, he was back up encouraging her to keep moving.

Not a minute later, a brick building came into full view. A concrete silo in front flagged a large metal door with an equally oversized lock.

They scrambled to it while Lauren prayed for sanctuary.

Jaden stood, angling his shoulder toward the door. Stepping back, he rammed forward with the fury of a steam engine. The door buckled, but stopped short of opening. He grunted and rubbed his shoulder.

"We need something...," he said before disappearing around the side of the building.

A few moments later the front door opened and an arm, which felt more like a steel band, swept her inside. She stumbled forward, falling against Jaden to catch her balance.

He planted his shoulder against the door, struggling to close it against the elements.

Lauren spun around, grabbed the sliding metal latch, and bolted the lock as soon as it lined up.

She turned, leaned against the door, and found herself once again inside Jaden's arms. He was out of breath, she could tell by the pulsing rhythm of his chest. She was soaked to the core, and the heat from his glorious body pressing against hers was a beacon of warmth. Lauren allowed the warmth to calm her as his arms encircled her waist and pulled her in tighter, until her breath slowed to a normal rhythm.

"Do you think we're alone?" she asked.

"For now." Jaden took off his shirt, once more revealing his perfectly toned abs. He squeezed the water out and used it to gently wipe mud from her face.

His thumb traced her cheekbone, sending warmth swirling through her.

She didn't move, couldn't move. She could only stand there spellbound, waiting for the magic to break.

"We just have to wait until the storm blows over. There are basic supplies here and secure communication equipment. This should be safe," he said.

A crack of thunder returned Lauren's full focus. He might've saved them from the storm, but that wasn't the only thing they were running from. Besides, if she stood there with him any longer she wouldn't be able to resist him. "We'll see about that."

His hand found hers, and next thing she knew she was being led into a large room. Teal blue paint chipped off plaster walls. The furniture, old and sparse, looked to be original and about as soft as a tree trunk, but it was something. She tested a chair and found it to be as hard as it looked.

Maybe she was being silly, but she expected high-tech equipment, a few couches, and a desk. "This isn't it, is it? I mean, we're kind of out in the open, aren't we?"

Jaden smiled as he guided her toward a floor-to-ceiling cabinet.

Concrete floors were cold but dry. Her gaze landed on a fireplace. And, glory of glories, there was wood cut and neatly stacked beside it just waiting for them. It was probably a prop for a tour guide, but she didn't care. It looked real enough. "Can we light a fire?"

"This isn't it. And don't worry about this location. No matter what, I'll keep you safe. Your brother needs you." He opened the cabinet and removed shelving.

If she looked really closely, she could see a small button in the back, which looked like nothing more than a paint splatter.

Jaden pushed the spot, and the back wall of the cabinet opened like a scene out of an Indiana Jones film.

Lauren stepped inside and felt as though she'd been transported to another world. A couple of desks, butted against each other, centered the room. A wall in back was filled with high-tech-looking equipment, none of which Lauren recognized. It looked like the ultimate man cave, complete with a wood-burning fireplace and worn couch.

"This fireplace works." He brought a thin wire

and a hand towel. "No one will see the smoke coming from the chimney in this downpour."

Crossing to the supplies, he pulled batteries from the radio. Organizing wood into a small teepee, he said, "Grab me that broomstick over there." He pointed to the corner.

Lauren brought over the small whiskbroom, unsure of what he planned to do with this odd collection of supplies. "No matches?"

"Don't need any."

He pulled out a handful of stiff fibers and laced them through the wood. Attaching wire to each battery terminal, he touched the ends of the bare wires together next to the tinder. Sparks ignited the broom fibers on the first try. He blew out breaths in short bursts while fanning the flame.

When the old wood started to crackle and hiss, he leaned back on his heels. His slow smile stretched full lips over beautiful, white teeth. She could stare at him forever when he smiled.

"Is this part of your training?" she asked, wondering if using his charm was also nothing more than a weapon.

"Yes." If Jaden was being honest, he'd admit how badly he wanted to lay her down right then and there, feel her silky legs wrap around his waist and bury himself inside her.

The moment crashed when he really looked at her. She was dripping wet, her teeth chattering behind a slight smile on her purple lips.

"Maybe these wet clothes will dry out soon."

Crossing to the couch, he grabbed a dry blanket. "Take 'em off."

She peeled off her soaked clothes before wrapping the blanket around her. He turned his back to give her privacy.

"Okay, you can look now," she said before motioning toward the gash on her forehead. "How bad is it?"

"Lay down on the couch," he instructed. He settled next to her with a bottled water and a handful of paper towels. He poured the water over the cut on her forehead, carefully dabbing it a moment later with the clean towel.

He opened the emergency medical kit they kept stocked at the safe house and located a small packet of Bacitracin. "This antibiotic gel will keep your cut from getting infected." He placed a thin trail of the gel on her forehead before bandaging her with fresh gauze and medical tape. "Better," he said, satisfied with himself, battling the urge to lean over and kiss her sweet skin.

"Thank you."

"Now to see what's going on." Jaden hoped someone from ManTech hadn't tipped off the bad guys off to his location at the condo. The once-laughable idea that there could be a mole in the agency wasn't funny anymore. Then again, Helena craved revenge so badly she could be making mistakes, leaving a trail that anyone could capitalize on. Camila Menendez was smart. She'd lead Jaden and Smith into an ambush. A woman like her would take advantage of any weakness, any crack in the system.

Jaden needed to signal Gunner again, and they needed to be ready for anything. He returned to the fire a moment later with a small laptop he'd retrieved from one of the desks. This signal was the most secure. It would be scrambled from the safe house, making it even more difficult for the cartel to locate him. If someone from the agency was the problem, Jaden would find out soon enough.

"Are you contacting your boss?" Lauren stretched before tightening the covers around her.

"I need to figure out a way to get you off this island," he said.

She shook her head furiously. "Not without Max."

Despite her fears, she looked peaceful and safe, cocooned in the blanket. Another peak of light elbowed into his dark soul.

Jaden pulled out the SIM card he'd taken from Beady Eyes and placed it into the computer. It would take the system a while to hack into it. They might find answers.

Lauren's hopeful expression dropped, replaced by another that nailed Jaden's gut. Like she'd come in to contact with men like these a little too often.

"What about your agency? You said people are being targeted? How do you know who you can trust?" she asked.

"There's only one way to find out and that's contact my boss. I'll keep you safe no matter what. You know that, right?" Big eyes stared at him before she nodded.

He typed in the code, sending the signal for a meeting with Gunner. The message would let his boss know Jaden had made it to the safe house. Jaden hoped it wasn't a mistake to give his location to the man a second time. He closed down the laptop and secured it back into its spot.

He then fanned Lauren's clothes on the hearth. "These should be dry in no time."

"It's nice to be warm and dry again." She paused before locking gazes with him. "Will your guy come here to meet us?"

"He was probably on his way already." Jaden cleaned and dried his Glock before moving to a cabinet full of ammunition. "We'll be ready for whoever walks through that door."

A flash of fear darkened her features and he had a

feeling it was more than just this situation. "Everything okay?"

She stared at the door like a ghost might walk through, or something worse...an abuser. She stood up and moved to the fire.

"I hate being afraid of anything," she admitted. "But I especially hate watching doors."

CHAPTER 14

"WHAT HAPPENED?" Looking at Lauren standing next to the fire—her sweet face, the rosy hue to her cheeks, those pink lips—stirred emotions deep in Jaden's chest. His feelings were running deeper than a fleeting attraction. That made her more dangerous than the storm, or the thugs chasing them through it, or the possibility of someone at ManTech turning.

"When Max and me were little...it might be easier to say what didn't happen. Neglect? Check. Abuse? Check. Our mother worked late hours when she had a job. There was a man who lived downstairs who used to try to get in the door. Max would push a chair against the knob. One time Max made an anonymous call to the police pretending to be one of our neighbors because the guy got inside and dragged me away from Max. My brother was too quick thinking to let anything too bad happen. But we always had to be on our toes. There were other times when our mother would come home and go on some rampage about the house not being clean enough. I took the brunt of those times," she said with a shrug. "Bruises heal. The psychological stuff is much worse. Max stopped anyone from violating me but mom was physical. Once she got started hitting us it seemed hard for her to stop."

Jaden ran his finger along a scar on her forearm. "She did this to you?"

"It's nothing." She sounded embarrassed for sharing.

"That's not true and I'm sorry." No one had been able to break down Jaden's iron walls or reach the core of him. But Lauren, beautiful, sweet, innocent Lauren kept hammering at the casing.

Jaden went to the small fridge filled with emergency supplies and brought back more bottled water, pain relievers, and canned fruit.

"These should help with your shoulder," he said, placing a couple ibuprofen in her hand. He had no such magic for the bruises on her insides. The thought roiled his gut. Was that why she didn't trust him? Men? His fingers clenched around the water bottle. He forced them to relax. He wouldn't let another man hurt her. She was safe. Safe and brave and beautiful.

"Why own a flower shop?" he asked.

"I specialize in native and wildflower arrangements. I guess after my childhood I wanted to surround myself with as much beauty as I could." She looked down. "My mother used to refer to herself as being wild. I always thought of that as a bad thing. That's what I came from so maybe I was wild, too. And then I stood in front of a field of Bluebonnets in the spring. I must've been around sixteen, still in high school. I'd never seen so much beauty. And then I realized they were wild, too."

Her golden gaze pierced into him.

Jaden's heart squeezed.

"Your friend back on the beach. Were you two close?" She turned the tables.

"As close as two people can be when they work in this business." It was a copout. He knew it and hoped she didn't pick up on it.

He checked progress on the computer. Nothing yet.

Her gaze locked onto his when he glanced up. "You like working alone all the time?"

Damn. She did.

"It never bothered me before. Besides, we don't completely work alone. We usually have a couple guys on the job at a time. We don't interface much except for work."

"Sounds lonely. You don't know who you'll work with beforehand? When you're walking into a situation? How do you separate the good guys from the bad? How do you know not to shoot one of your own?" She clasped her hands together.

"First of all, you don't walk in shooting unless you have to. Second, you look them in the eyes. Third, sometimes we're told in advance. We focus on the objective, not each other." It sounded cold and lonely when he heard himself talk about his work. It used to provide and adrenaline rush but that had been ebbing lately.

"The black in that guy's eyes back at the condo. I saw pure evil when he looked at me. It was the same with the guy on the beach," she said.

"You can't fake true wickedness. And you can't fake good. It's either there, or it isn't." Did she see black when you looked in his eyes when they'd first met?

With her background, he figured she saw black in most people's eyes.

"Why do they trust you? Your agency train you how to convince them you're bad, too?" she continued.

"You can't train evil. It might be fleeting, but it's there or it isn't," he said.

"Why don't they make you guys?"

Make? Did her ideas of his work come from the movies? "It's not like that. Not at all like the movies make it out to be."

"Then how?" She fisted the knot on her blanket.

"I have to be better at my job than they are at

theirs. I have to convince them I'm on their side." He wanted to open up to her, tell her things he didn't normally tell anyone. But how could he?

"And your friend on the beach? What about him?" she asked.

"Look. I had history with Bryce running all the way back to our days in the military. We were as close as any two guys can be who work in jobs like ours. He's dead now. End of story." He was the closest thing to a friend Jaden had. The two of them had never even been out for a casual beer. It had always been all too easy for Jaden to close himself off from the rest of the world, to use his job as an excuse as to why he did. His excuses seemed flimsy when he talked to Lauren.

"But are you okay?" she asked, her concern bringing out the copper tone in her golden eyes.

There she was, asking that question again. Who was really every *okay*? What did *okay* even mean?

"I'll survive." He heard the hollowness in his own words. He didn't like it.

"For how long, Jaden?"

Hell if he knew. He didn't answer.

"How did you get that bullet hole in your shoulder?" The knot became suddenly interesting to her.

"I trusted the wrong person."

"Is that why you're so cautious now?" Her gaze didn't falter even though his heart did.

A piercing shriek sounded from one of the laptops.

Jaden hopped up and moved to the screen.

"Gunner's here."

A THIN MAN, average height, who looked to be early forties with white-streaked hair slipped in.

Jaden stepped forward and offered a handshake. "I've been worried about you."

Green eyes framed by thick black glasses scanned Lauren. He nodded, shaking water from his soaked clothes. "I could say the same."

"Me? Nah. I seem to have the unique ability to be the only one who walks away from a gunfight. Where the hell have you been?" Jaden asked.

Blood stained Gunner's overcoat. His expression weary. His head shook. "We lost another soldier today. We were ambushed while trying to get to the condo."

"What happened?" Jaden asked, concerned he'd done the wrong thing in bringing Lauren here.

"Someone's been a step behind me everywhere I go." Gunner glanced around and Jaden realized the implication.

Jaden tucked Lauren further behind him. "Helena's becoming reckless. She might be leading them to our door."

"Makes sense." Gunner's expression didn't change. Instead of commenting, he moved to the fire. "May I?"

"Of course. You know about Bryce?"

Gunner's unfocused gaze started away from the fire as a pained expression dropped his brow. "Yes. I do. We lost another first-rate soldier."

"He was a good guy," Jaden agreed.

"You okay?" Gunner asked.

"Right as rain." What was it with everyone today? Jaden was a big boy. He'd seen other men die on assignment. Right next to him. In his arms. Why did people suddenly look at him with concern?

Gunner frowned. "People like you and me don't have many real friends, do we?"

Jaden cleared his throat. He didn't want to focus on the deficiencies in his life right now. He needed information. More than anything, Jaden needed to know if he could protect Lauren. He pointed to the screen. "I took a SIM card off one of them. Maybe we can get photos and figure out where their headquarters is located."

"Might be difficult to break the encryption, but that could be very helpful if we can," Gunner admitted.

"What happened to you earlier? You were supposed to be on the beach." If he had been, Bryce might be sitting here enjoying a beer right now instead of lying dead out there, God knew where.

"Only a select few knew where we were going this morning. I have to believe one of them set us up. I can't prove anything. There's only the body count and my suspicion." Jaden had known it, and still the confirmation from Gunner hit hard.

It was becoming a virus in his agency. He eased his grip on his weapon, tucked it away, and moved to the fire, taking a seat next to Gunner. "What happened to communication? I know Bryce would've signaled for help."

"Someone jammed our frequency. They anticipated our arrival. They led us to what was supposed to be a safe house where we were—"

"Camila Menendez." Jaden rocked his head. "I'd bet money she's behind this."

Gunner nodded. "At one point I had to toss my cell. They must've recovered it and hacked into it. I'm sure that's how they tracked my every move."

Gunner looked as tired and strained as Jaden felt. "You think they got anything out of Tim while they had him?"

"It would explain how they're anticipating our every move." Gunner motioned toward the computer screen. "Maybe we'll get something off the SIM."

"I know one thing's certain, Max might just be the key." Was this whole mission doomed to fail from the get-go?

The computer pinged.

Gunner moved toward it. "Looks like we got something."

Jaden was already standing behind him.

"We can retrace this guy's steps by pinning the locations he made calls from." Gunner's fingers danced across the keyboard, and a map of the island popped up in the left-hand corner.

A cluster of red dots populated the map.

Jaden sighed sharply. "I know the area. It'll be crawling with Menendez's people."

The chance to bust Camila got his blood pumping.

Gunner's expression tensed. "I got intel yesterday about a safe house they have here. It's the most logical place to stash Max." He pointed to a spot on the map. "It'll be dangerous."

Lauren dropped to her knees. "Does this mean what I think? Max is here?"

"Most likely," Jaden supplied.

"Is he..."

"Alive? I believe so. And he's not far. We have a weather window. We'll have to move fast. I'll alert Gabriel." Gunner pulled a new cell from the cabinet and started punching numbers.

Jaden's stress factor hit a hard run. Normally, an extraction would get his blood going. In this case, it felt risky.

"On the phone, it sounded like they hit him with a

bat or something." Lauren's brown-gold eyes were wide.

Gunner's gaze bounced off the floor and back. "As soon as we extract him, he'll have the best possible medical care available. We'll do everything we can to help him heal."

"You're not saying...he *will* survive...won't he?" Tears flooded her eyes.

Jaden's heart squeezed at the panic in her voice, the bravery she showed.

"From what we know about Menendez so far, I believe he'll be okay. They don't want him dead just yet. They won't have been easy on him. He'll have a long road ahead to heal. From everything I hear, he's a fighter," Gunner said.

"Thank you for helping my brother. I know he doesn't deserve it after what he's become, but thank you," Lauren said, tiny droplets staining her cheeks.

"There's something else I learned this morning." Gunner shifted an ominous gaze to Jaden.

"Go ahead and say whatever you need to. I trust her." Jaden stood behind his vow.

"The Marshal he was talking to has been killed," Gunner said.

"Max was turning state's witness?" Lauren asked. Gunner nodded.

She turned to Jaden. "Did you know?"

"That intel wasn't part of your file." He shook his head. "You think Menendez figured it out?"

It would make sense. Revenge would be a good reason for the kidnapping. Making Max's family suffer before killing him was right up their alley.

"Can't say for sure," Gunner said.

Anger had Jaden clenching his fists before he realized he was doing it and stopped. As much as Max might've been a criminal he deserved a chance to make his life right. "Does Helena know any of this?"

Gunner glanced from Lauren and back to Jaden again. "It's possible."

Jaden didn't state the obvious fact that people rarely ever got out once they went in this deep. There were two paths for those like Max, prison or death. "Did Max owe money?"

"We have no intel about debts." Gunner turned to Lauren. "Excuse me for saying, but your recent financial records indicate you've taken out loans and cleaned out your bank account."

Her angry eyes flashed. "Then you already know I brought one hundred and fifty thousand dollars to the island with me."

"Sorry for the intrusion." Gunner's tone was genuine but Lauren didn't seem to take the invasion of her privacy lightly.

Lauren's lips thinned. She didn't speak.

"I'd say it's just part of the job, but I can imagine how this must appear and feel to an outsider," Gunner said regretfully.

"Degrading. And I didn't do anything wrong." She

held onto the blanket tightly. "If my brother wanted out, why didn't he just disappear? He had to know these men were dangerous."

"You go rouge on these guys, they tend to go after your family," Jaden said quietly. His words seemed to strike Lauren like a physical blow.

"He stuck around to protect me." She lowered her gaze. "Sounds like something the old Max would do."

Gunner took off his raingear. "If someone like Ruiz wanted his territory they might take him in order to extort money."

"I'm certain Menendez's boys were on the beach," Jaden said.

Gunner paused for one thoughtful moment. He glanced at his phone. "Gabriel will be here in a minute. Says he has something to show you."

Lauren twisted her hands together. "Could they be after me to hurt my brother even more?"

Jaden took her hand to reassure her. "I'm afraid so. If he gave them any indication hurting you would be his ultimate pain."

"Our intel says you don't have any other family," Gunner said quietly.

Lauren's back teeth clenched.

CHAPTER 15

LAUREN DIDN'T TALK about the past with anyone. She'd told Jaden more in the short time she'd known him than any other human being. She didn't tell any of her employees at the flower shop. Or customers even though she made arrangements for their tables for holidays and heard all about the big meals they had planned and the family and laughter they anticipated.

If it would help Max, she would have to. She took in a fortifying breath. "There's no one else. I mean, they could be alive. Who really knows? I'd be the last one to be told."

Gunner's green eyes darkened with what looked like sorrow when he said, "I'm sorry to be the one to tell you this. Our intelligence says your mother passed away five years ago."

A few tears welled in Lauren's eyes. Pain that

shouldn't be there pierced her insides anyway. It shouldn't matter that her mother was gone. It shouldn't hit Lauren this hard. After all, her mother was a stranger. They hadn't seen in each other in more than a decade and the woman certainly hadn't been around when she was growing up. At least not sober. And yet, she was still her mother. Lauren fought the urge to release the emotion burning her chest.

The rain pattern shifted to a rhythmic pulse as Jaden pulled weapons from cabinets, tucked them in his waistband, and handed others to Gunner. He looked ready to wage war.

"Are you sure it was her?" she asked.

"We're confident. She'd been sick for a few years leading to her death. She lived in a trailer park in rural Arkansas with a man identified as Jeb Stanton. Does that name sound familiar?"

Lauren shook her head, steeling herself against the tsunami of emotion building.

Gunner continued, "We couldn't find your father."

Tears fell. Lauren took in a fortifying breath. She was determined not to lose it. She'd been expecting news like this about her parents someday. Confirmation hurt.

Next thing she knew Jaden was by her side, his comforting arm around her waist.

"Good luck finding him," Lauren said. "God knows I tried."

"On your birth certificate, your mother wrote—"

She pushed out a little puff of air. "Mike Mouse. I know. She had a fixation for all things Mickey Mouse from her childhood. Had quite the sense of humor didn't she?"

"We don't have to do this if you don't want to." Jaden's comforting arm tightened around her.

"I can't ignore it forever," she responded.

"She ever talk about your father?" he asked.

"Said he ran out on us before she had time to tell him she was pregnant with me. Max is the oldest. So, no, I never met my father. He doesn't even know I'm alive. He might as well be dead for all I know of him."

"She didn't mention his real name?" Jaden continued.

"Never."

"Max never mentioned it either?" Gunner asked.

"We're only two years apart. He was a baby when our father left. Why?" she asked defensively.

Gunner pursed his lips. "I know this is difficult to talk about. But it's important. We don't know what information might be critical to figuring this thing out. It's a long shot, I know, that your parents could be connected to this. I had to ask."

Were it not for his genuine look of concern Lauren might have been more upset with where this was going.

The only thing rooting her to reality was Jaden.

With his strong arm wrapped around her waist, she could handle anything thrown her way.

"These guys kill if you happen to stand on the wrong side of the street. Life means nothing to them. But why go after Lauren? She has nothing to do with her brother," Jaden said.

Gunner nodded his agreement. "It wouldn't take much to agitate them. Menendez is especially ruthless. He might have taken Max's leaving personally and decided to get revenge before killing Max."

Jaden's forehead creased even more with concerned lines. "They seem especially intent on finding her. The only other reason I can think of is if they're planning on forcing her to use her shop in order to launder money to the U.S.?"

Gunner seemed locked in thought for a long moment. "It's possible. We've seen it before."

What have you gotten yourself into, Max? Without warning, tears streamed and, for once, she didn't fight them.

A few moments later, she felt herself being repositioned until her face burrowed in Jaden's chest. He murmured soothing words into her hair. "Take your time. This is a lot to absorb. I'm right here. I won't leave you."

Gathering her strength, she wiped her tears and looked toward Gunner. "When do we leave?"

"We'll take you home as soon as we get weather clearance."

She shook her head empathetically. "I'm not going home. I'm going with you to get Max."

"No can do. It's too dangerous," Jaden said quickly.

"How can I even think about going home?"

"Gunner and I will get Max. You'll stay here. We'll bring him back, and you'll go home together."

"I need to be there to see he's okay," she stated.

Jaden pulled her to the side. Anger flashed in his eyes. "Too risky."

"This is my problem. He's my brother. I think I realize what we're facing. I have the bumps and bruises to prove it."

"We don't even know what we're facing. If there's a leak from my agency, we could be ambushed again," Jaden said, anger pulsing off him in waves. "Did you hear Gunner before? Did you see the blood on his coat?"

"I have to go with you. I don't expect you to understand. But information is leaking on your side and you can't guarantee my safety if you leave me here. The only way you can watch over me is if I'm with you."

Jaden's face twisted. He looked to be contemplating her words. It was true. No one could deny it.

Gunner's cell buzzed. Lauren froze.

Gunner's gaze shifted from his phone to Jaden. "Helena's out front with Gabriel."

"Helena's here? I thought she was in the States." Jaden sounded startled.

"Guess not." Gunner shot a look.

Jaden's response was a quick nod. "I should've known. Must be what Gabriel wanted to show me."

"You need to decide what you're going to do with her." Gunner's head inclined toward Lauren.

"She stays," he barked.

"No. I don't. Besides, you guys have been talking about a mole or whatever. How am I supposed to defend myself against one of yours? Especially if they come here?"

Anguish and frustration scored Jaden's forehead. "Dammit."

Gunner dragged his hand across the stubble on his chin. "She's right. We don't know how they're staying ahead of us, but they are. She might be vulnerable here. The only way to ensure her safety is to keep our eyes on her at all times."

Jaden grabbed a jacket and tossed dry clothes to her. "Fine. She goes. But she stays inside the vehicle."

Lauren wouldn't argue. She took the clothes and dressed.

"I'm ready," Lauren said when she emerged from the bathroom. Jaden's hand closed on hers.

He didn't say a word as he led her out the door. His dark, brooding expression tied knots in her stomach. He didn't need to speak for her to know what was on his mind. This mission might be a death trap.

Lauren climbed into the back of Gunner's SUV at Jaden's urging. His heft blocked her view of the driver until she sat down and found her seatbelt being strapped around her. "I got it. Thanks."

Her nerves would've been completely unhinged by now, but physical contact with Jaden kept her a notch below panic. He'd wedged himself in the middle seat, and his thigh brushed against hers. Electricity hummed between them.

Her first glimpse of the man in the front passenger seat almost made her smile. Were all operatives seriously this good looking? Gabriel had sandy-brown hair and the greenest eyes. She guessed he'd stand an inch or two shorter than Jaden. He was almost as muscular.

Gabriel turned around, smiled, and winked. "Nasty weather today."

Jaden's shoulder came forward, blocking more of her view. "There's no good weather for what we're about to do."

She strained to get a good look at Helena.

Huge dark brown eyes looked at her from the rearview. Long thick lashes framed them.

"You've had quite a day," her smooth voice said. "We'll get your brother out of there."

A band of jealousy tightened around Lauren's heart.

Jaden's muscles tensed. "When we do, you and I need to have a sit down, Helena."

The dark beautiful eyes blinked. Dark. Beautiful. Dangerous.

Lauren saw a flash of rage behind those eyes.

"I've been watching this place today. Hoping. They weren't there this morning. They must've brought him when things went south at the beach," Helena said.

The drive was short. Fifteen to twenty minutes max. The house was located in the center of town.

"What now?" Lauren quietly asked Jaden.

"We assess." He paused a beat. "But you wait."

"I didn't ask for any of this. I wish my brother hadn't dragged me into it too. But I'm here. I don't plan to sit in this car while you guys risk your lives."

"We're trained. You're not."

Motion from the driver's seat caught Lauren's attention. Helena turned in the seat with the butt of a gun toward Lauren. "She can use my backup weapon. We need all the fire power we can get."

Jaden's hand covered Helena's, and a tidal wave of jealousy rolled up, burning through Lauren's chest.

"We don't risk civilians," he said, his eyes flashing a warning.

The face that came with the cat-like eyes was staggering to look at. Her hair, dark and radiant, framed an almond-shaped face. Sultry auburn streaks could be seen around the edges. She shifted her head slightly as she spoke, and light seeped in, barely settling on each strand, revealing a brilliant shine breaking through everywhere the storm's darkness didn't obscure.

"Like it or not, she's involved. Her help might just mean the difference between life and death."

Jaden's body, poised for battle, stiffened. His fists clenched. "I said—"

"We have enough manpower without her," Gunner interrupted.

Helena's gaze intensified. "Leave her in the car and someone has to stay back to watch her. We'll be more vulnerable if we split up. Besides, we've already lost five men. It's not prudent to risk more. I'll cover her inside."

Impatience shot from Jaden's glare. "Then she comes with me."

The house they watched wasn't bigger than a shack. There was almost no yard, the buildings sandwiched right next to each other. Jaden scouted the area carefully. Lauren followed his gaze to an eighteenth century church across the street. Its whitewashed walls offered a hint of light in the darkness surrounding them. He glanced toward her, and then his gaze shifted back to the church.

She nodded. If it goes awry, meet him in the chapel.

Helena's gaze locked onto Lauren, making her uncomfortable. "They say he has a tattoo of a dragon on his neck. The man who killed Tim," she said, anger causing her voice to tremble.

The front door of the shack opened as a black SUV roared up.

"Get down!" Jaden said as he folded forward. One of Menendez's top men had that tattoo.

Lauren slid until her knees butted against the back of the driver's seat.

Their car was hidden from view, but no one seemed in the mood to take unnecessary chances.

"They're most likely moving him again," Jaden whispered.

"If they take him somewhere else, we'll never find him," Lauren said, desperation a lead weight sinking to the pit of her stomach.

"This is good. We don't know what we're up against inside the shack. This way, we can follow them. Strike when we're ready," he said.

The door to the SUV opened and closed, and then it was on the move again.

Helena didn't immediately move. "They're watching. Two big men at the front door."

"Patience. We'll catch up to them," Jaden confidently said.

Lauren's stomach lining was braided from stress.

"How do we know they have Max?"

CHAPTER 16

"WE DON'T FOR SURE. This could be a decoy," Jaden said to Lauren. His words weren't exactly reassuring.

Gunner leaned forward. "I'm betting they're moving him. They'll want to take advantage of the break in weather. They don't normally leave a witness in the same place for long."

Lauren wished she felt more reassured.

"They've gone back inside," Helena said, starting the engine. "It's safe."

She wheeled left, the same way the SUV had gone moments before

"How will we find them?" Lauren asked.

"Easy, they'll be the only other car on the street," Helena said, her slight accent almost a purr.

A stab of jealousy Lauren had no right to own hit her.

Jaden's left hand covered hers. Her body ached to

be in his arms again. His right hand palmed his gun, reminding her of the danger they were in.

In the front seat, Gabriel shouldered a weapon that looked like an assault rifle. Lauren knew very little about guns, but this one seemed especially threatening. Gunner had his weapon out and ready.

The weight of just how deadly this situation was sent a shot of adrenaline rocketing through her.

"Turn right," Gabriel said. "Now!"

Helena jammed the wheel in time for Lauren to see brake lights ahead as the other SUV turned down another side street.

"There! I see it," Lauren said, she held onto the gun Helena had given her with shaky hands.

After a few twists and turns, Helena roared up behind the SUV. The SUV hit the brakes hard, and the Range Rove slammed into its bumper. Thankfully, the jolt wasn't strong enough to deploy the air bags. Gunfire ensued as the SUV fishtailed in front of them.

Helena maneuvered around the left side of the vehicle. Blacked out windows made identifying anyone inside impossible. Jaden bolted into action next to Gunner, firing his weapon.

Tat. Tat. Tat. The noise was so loud Lauren's eardrums rang.

The passenger side window shattered.

The other SUV jerked right.

Damn.

Helena hit the brake and slammed the SUV into Reverse as Jaden slipped out the door.

"Bring them to me," was all he said before he disappeared around the block.

Helena hit the gas so hard the tires spun, trying to find traction on the wet concrete. They caught, and the SUV jerked forward. She rounded the corner and caught up to the other SUV. She came up on its right side, forcing it into a left turn.

Helena forced another turn, and the knot in Lauren's stomach tightened. She saw the minute Jaden stepped from a building.

His shot must've been dead on. The other SUV jerked sideways before running head on into a building.

All three operatives descended from the other SUV.

The scene slowed to a crawl for Lauren. Bullets flew. Sounds warped. Her heart stayed in her throat.

By the time she gathered her senses, a man was being pulled from the SUV. His frame was thin, his body limp, but she'd recognize her brother anywhere. Relief washed over her until she got a good look on his face.

Jaden climbed in the back, holding Max. "Go!"

The others slid inside Gunner's SUV. Helena stopped at the door, aimed her weapon, and shot. An explosion rocked the pavement. For a split-second, Lauren feared they'd been hit.

Jaden's hand covered hers reassuringly. "Max is safe."

The drive back to the safe house seemed to take forever. Max might be safe, but he was unconscious. Fear gripped Lauren. He had to be okay.

As they settled her brother inside headquarters, Gunner said, looking concerned, "Think you can rest until air transportation arrives? You both look exhausted."

She shot a worried look toward Jaden. Gunner, Gabriel, and Helena seemed honest enough, but she wasn't exactly trained to pick out the good from the bad. Could they trust anyone?

Everyone in Jaden's agency was trained to make people believe they were someone else. Hadn't Jaden said something about eyes giving it away? Wouldn't a man who'd been trained to hide his identity be skilled at tricking people?

"Gunner's right. You need rest," Jaden said. His tense posture said he was poised for battle. "I've got a few of my own wounds to dress. Plus, I need time to think about this."

"Only if you promise to wake me if there's any change in my brother's condition," she said through a yawn, checking on Max again. Arguing would do no good but she highly doubted she'd be able to sleep.

Max's face, battered and bruised, sent her heart into a free fall.

"You have my word," Jaden said.

"Now sleep. I'll be here when you wake up. Right next to you." Jaden was telling her he'd keep an eye on things. She knew firsthand how he could handle himself in pretty much every situation. He'd collected the bumps and bruises to prove it.

"We need to get back out before the weather turns again," Helena said, looking antsy.

"I know how bad you want these guys. Believe me, I do too," Jaden said.

Her mouth twisted in anger. "No one wants the man who killed Tim dead more than me. Those men didn't do it. I need to go back to the house and watch. He's close by and I can feel it."

"The dragon tattoo?" Jaden asked.

Gabriel eased off the desk he'd been sitting on. "I'll go with her."

Jaden shook his hand. "Be safe out there. Report back when you can."

The door closed and Jaden's attention turned to Lauren. "You need sleep and we'll have to wait a while until it's safe to be in the air."

"And a hot meal. A warm bed. If a plane can fly, you'll wake me up immediately, right?" she asked, stifling another yawn.

"As soon as the storm breaks, we'll get you both out of here. You're going home."

Home? Where was that anymore?

Home felt a lot like Jaden.

A FEW HOURS of sleep and dry clothes made all the difference in the world to Lauren. She woke to find Jaden's arms wrapped around her, her back pressed against the crook of his arm, and her head resting on his shoulder.

The moment she stirred, his eyes flew open, and his arms tightened around her protectively.

"I'm okay. Just thirsty. I didn't mean to wake you," she said.

He repositioned, loosening his grip. "Don't get up. Stay here. Rest. I'll get water for you. I want you to save your strength. We have a long journey home later."

As soon as he moved, she missed the feel of his strong, warm body against hers. "Has my brother's condition changed?"

Jaden shook his head. "He's stable."

"I can hardly imagine what it'll be like to have my brother back. I mean….he left ages ago. I don't really know him anymore," she said.

"Your brother's safe. You're safe. Nothing else matters," Jaden said, returning with a fresh bottle of water for her.

"Because of you, I'm alive." She wondered about Jaden. Who kept him safe?

She heard rhythmic breathing coming from the makeshift bed Gunner had made.

"Speaking of my brother and his safety, what about the hospital? I mean, will anyone be able to get to him there?" she asked in a whisper.

"If he's turning State's evidence, then he'll receive the best possible protection and care. Believe me. They'll do everything in their power to keep him alive to testify. It's not for the reason you want or because they care but the result is the same," he said, taking his seat next to her again.

She leaned in closer to him, wanting to be as near as possible. "Can I stay at the hospital with him?"

"You can visit. He's in critical condition which probably means a trip straight to ICU, so we'll have visiting hours to consider. Other than that, you should be fine. We'll have to figure out a way to disguise you."

"Meaning it's best if they don't see me going in?"

"It's just a precaution. We don't know who might be watching, and until he breaks consciousness we don't have a clue as to what all this is really about. Everything we said before was just guessing. Max is the key," he said.

Lauren's stomach dropped. "You don't think there's a chance he won't—"

"He'll be fine. He'll get the new lease on life he needs when this is over. A new identity. A new location. A real job. This is his best chance to start over if he's serious about wanting a new life," Jaden said.

"Why not do that before? I mean, couldn't he have

turned himself in to the government?" She felt his body tense and it dawned on her. Jaden had said it before. She would have been in danger. Plus, if Max turned state's evidence he would have to give up everyone he knew before. Which was basically her. She wondered if that could be the reason he'd called. Did he want her advice before making the commitment? Did he want to say good-bye? Guilt sat heavy on her chest.

Lauren hadn't considered the possibility that once he testified she might never see him again. The sadness of the thought hit her hard.

One day at a time. For now, she'd be grateful her brother received the second chance Jaden's didn't. "You told me about your brother. Do you have parents out there somewhere waiting to hear from you? Or other siblings?"

"There's no one." His words came out calm, like he was used to life on his own. Lauren could relate on so many levels.

"Can I ask a personal question?" She didn't expect him to answer, but it would be nice if he'd give her something, another reason to trust him.

"Go ahead."

She issued a breath and went for it. "Is Jaden Dean your real name?"

"It is now." There was no conviction in his voice.

"You don't remember your real name, or you don't tell people?"

"There a difference?" Had he gone so deep under cover that he'd forgotten who he really was? She'd read that happened to officers.

"You told me to trust you and I did. I still do. But I don't even know your name. I know next to nothing about you. It makes me think you don't trust me. Do you?" she asked.

"Look. My parents died in a car crash not long after my brother was killed. I had a grandmother who took me in. She lived long enough to see me graduate high school. From there I signed up for the military," he said, looking pained from the admission.

And toughened up? Became so tough no one could ever get close to you? Yet, she felt surprisingly close to him. How was it even possible? She knew so little about him. But she felt closer to him than she'd ever felt to anyone. Including Max. "You've lost so many people in your life. People you must've cared about."

He shrugged. "Not much loss really. My old man used to rough us up when we were little. Said he was teaching us how to be men."

"I'm so sorry." She touched his arm, ignoring the frissons of heat from contact.

"Don't be. It's how I know a real man would never hurt a person he loves," Jaden said in a hiss.

CHAPTER 17

WHOP. Whop. Whop.

The sweet sound of a UH60 Black Hawk came from the distance. Jaden squeezed Lauren's hand. He'd told her more about himself in the last fifteen minutes than he'd told anyone in his life. Strangely, it felt good to spill his secrets to her. The load pressing against his shoulders eased and light peaked into the darkness encasing his heart.

It was time to fly. Gunner stirred and checked his cell. Lauren checked on her brother.

"We're cleared. We gotta move fast." Gunner hopped to his feet. "We didn't get a chance to talk about this before. She'll need protection from here on out until we unravel this. Should I assign an agent?"

"You aren't saying you think they'll go after me back home, are you?" Lauren asked, eyes wide.

"I'm staying with her," Jaden said to Gunner before turning to Lauren. "It's a precaution. As soon as we know you're safe, you can have your life back. Until then, I'm not leaving your side, sweetheart."

Jaden wanted to tell her he would stay by her side forever. It was a promise he knew he couldn't keep. A man in his line of work couldn't commit to forever. And especially one who was in so deep that he'd lost all sense of normal life.

When he'd waxed nostalgic and reached out to Bryce back on the beach, he'd been killed. A couple of agents had families. Daniel Damon had a wife and daughter. He seemed the exception. Smith was gone, leaving behind a wife and kids. Helena would never be the same after losing Tim.

What kind of life was that?

If Jaden ever had rogue thoughts about wanting to settle down, Lauren was exactly his type. Smart. Beautiful. Brave. Incredibly sexy. And yet, it wouldn't be fair to risk her safety.

Lauren was already ensnared in a trap because of her brother. Her anguish was palpable. If she ached this much for her brother, how would she feel about her husband? Jaden's line of work would keep her in danger, too. Anyone tied to him would be threatened. A wife? Family? Jaden had never expected those things.

The life he'd built was meant for one.

Jaden figured the best he could do was keep

himself alive. He loved his work too much to consider changing professions. Besides, what else could he do? He was a soldier. And a damn good one. White picket fences and two point five kids had never been part of the plan. Lauren deserved both and anything else she wanted.

And yet, Jaden could admit that some of the thrill had been missing from his work lately. He'd been inside his head too much. Someday, when there were no more bad guys to fight or the fight drained from him, he'd retire and buy a fishing cabin. Then he'd fish until he couldn't stand the smell of bait anymore.

Lauren showed up and had him thinking about things he knew better than to expect. He wouldn't compromise her safety because he selfishly didn't want to leave her.

When Max woke, they would have the evidence they needed to put the Ruiz and Menendez bastards away for a very long time, and Jaden would disappear from her life forever.

His military training had taught him a thing or two about personal sacrifice. This was his job. Lauren was his asset. This was a protection detail, not a relationship.

So why did an invisible band tighten around his chest?

⁓

BEFORE LAUREN COULD UTTER the words, "Blue skies," Max was loaded and they were being whisked away on a Black Hawk helicopter bound for the States.

The noise from the rotors was deafening, and yet nothing could drown out the thoughts looping in her mind.

Her brother was safe.

She was heading home.

The experience seemed unreal to her now, like a dream, and she half expected to wake up any minute to realize none of it actually happened.

No one spoke on the long helicopter ride. Voices wouldn't be heard over the sound of rotors cutting through the air anyway. Lauren watched as a medical team worked on Max. Before long, he had an IV drip of antibiotics and enough pain meds to keep him comfortable.

Her hand rested in Jaden's the entire trip. He squeezed hers reassuringly from time to time.

They landed at Addison Airport in Dallas by eight o' clock in the evening. Lauren wanted to kiss the ground underneath her feet after touchdown.

An ambulance waited. As soon as they landed, the team transferred Max and disappeared.

When words could finally be heard over the roar of chopper blades, Jaden thanked Gunner.

"Where are you headed?" Jaden asked his boss.

"Back to D.C. to put some of these puzzle pieces together," Gunner said.

"You have the SIM card?" Jaden asked.

Gunner dipped his hand in his front pocket where he'd left it. "It's gone."

"Helena must've gotten to it. Damn. She's on a witch hunt and we need that evidence to turn over." Jaden swore again under his breath.

"I know she's angry, but I have to believe she'll be smart about this. I don't want you going after her yet," Gunner stated.

"For now, she's my priority," Jaden said, his hand pressed to Lauren's back. "Besides, Gabriel is with Helena. He'll keep things under control."

Lauren's heart practically danced, but then two words sunk in. *For now.* Her time with Jaden had an expiration date.

"Keep her safe. This'll all be sorted out soon," Gunner said.

A uniformed soldier interrupted them.

"These are yours," Gunner said, tossing a set of keys to Jaden, and motioning toward a parked sedan.

Lauren followed Jaden to the car. "Are we going to the hospital?"

"No. I'm taking you home first. They won't allow you to see him, and you've been through too much," he insisted. His tone left no room for argument. As much as she wanted to put up a fight she also realized he was right. Exhaustion wore thin and walking took great effort.

The ride home went by in a flash.

Lauren sighed as they reached her two-story brick townhouse at Preston and Royal inside half an hour.

"That's my place there," she pointed, "and we can pull in the attached garage."

Jaden didn't blink.

"You already know that, don't you?" What else did he know about her?

"It'll be best if we park close but not in your usual spot. There's a garage nearby that'll offer better coverage."

Of course, he knew where she lived. Her address —along with a host of other private information— would be in the same file the information about her parents could be found.

She hadn't even considered the possibility that the men she ran from might also have been watching her for a while. The thought of Beady Eyes or his partner or someone just like them keeping tabs on her sent a chill racing up her arms. This felt a lot like showing up for a fight wearing a blindfold. At least she had Jaden to count on, and she had come to depend on him for her survival.

"You don't think they'd come here, do you?" Lauren's heart pulsed in her throat.

"Anything's possible. We have to keep our guard up at all times." Jaden was probably being overly cautious, but she couldn't argue his logic. It was a smart play.

"We can park near the business over there. Their garages will be open and empty this time of night. Then we'll slip in and take a look." He drove up the garage to the fifth floor, parked strategically, and stared out the windshield.

Sitting there Lauren realized just how vulnerable she'd been. It was so easy to watch her front door. Anyone could sit there and track her comings and goings. Her routine could be memorized. A serial killer, stalker, or bum could keep track of all her movements from this spot without being detected. A chill raced through her. Lauren had never felt so exposed.

She looked at Jaden. His jaw was set, his gaze determined. He seemed to be running through and checking off all the possible dangers.

After a beat, his gaze shifted and met hers. "Okay," he said. "We can go now. Stick close by me."

He braided their fingers together as they walked, and Lauren momentarily imagined they were strolling home after dinner at a nearby restaurant, not secretly eyeing every person who passed by in case the person tried to kill them.

The pleasant picture erased completely when Jaden stopped at the front door. Blocking the way with his big frame, his gaze intently focused on her. "I'd better go in first."

A gasp escaped before Lauren could clamp it down. "You think someone might be inside?"

"I don't want to risk your safety to find out. It's better if you wait out here. You'll have a head start. You hear anything strange going on, and I want you to make a run for it. Don't stop." He put the keys to their vehicle in her hand.

"What about you, Jaden? How am I supposed to leave without knowing if you're okay?" she asked.

He took a step forward, pinning her to the wall of her landing. His mouth covered hers. His tongue, hot and needy, sent volts of want through her. All sense of time, place, and danger pooled around her feet in a knee melting kiss. Sensual pleasure heated her veins. A fierce need swirled warmth between her thighs.

Jaden pulled back, a smile tugged at the corner of his mouth. "That should do the trick for now."

There were those two words again...*for now.* They reminded her of the temporary nature of their relationship and the absurdity of it ever having a real chance. Too bad she was starting to believe she could spend more time with him. She gave herself a mental slap back to reality.

Jaden pulled the gun from his ankle holster.

Slowly, quietly, he opened the door, and Lauren's heart immediately dropped to the floor. She didn't need to step inside to see the place had been ransacked. Her couch had been overturned. The cushions slashed. Broken and scattered picture frames littered the floor.

"Ohmygosh. They've been here," she said in barely a whisper.

His gaze scanned every door, every surface, every possible hiding place. "Shhh. Stay here."

"Don't go in," she pleaded, tugging at his arm. She couldn't even think of him getting hurt, or worse.

Jaden didn't immediately break away from her, although his tense body language said he would. Instead, he turned to her and held her gaze. "I'll check it out. Make sure it's secure so you can get your things. Then you're coming to my place where I can protect you."

She swallowed, raw emotion threatening to drop her. "I'm going inside with you."

"Not this time. You stay put. I need you here to watch out for them. You make sure not a soul comes through this door. If anyone out there looks suspicious, scream as loud as you can."

He produced a small gun from his boot, took off the safety, and placed the weapon in her shaky palm.

"Look first, then shoot." The spark of determination in his eyes confirmed he meant what he said.

"But what if something happens to…"

His eyes glinted. "You're sexy when you're worried."

"Be careful." Sensual heat crawled up her neck, mixed with fear, but this was not the time for either.

"Take care of yourself until I come back for you," he said, pressing a kiss to her lips.

She forced her attention to the walkway outside. She couldn't think why anyone would come to her place. Except maybe for money. Did they think she'd hide it here instead of taking it with her?

Gun drawn, Jaden eased inside. One more time, he quietly instructed Lauren to stay back.

What felt like an eternity later, but in reality was only a few minutes, he returned and motioned her to join him.

In the kitchen, her table and chairs had been turned over. Cabinets had been emptied onto the floor where shards of glass mixed with broke bits of bone China.

"Everything's here. It doesn't look like anything's missing, just destroyed. Why would they do that?" she asked.

Jaden kept guard near the door. "At first I thought maybe they were looking for something. But now, I think they're sending a message."

"To me? What did I do to them?" she asked.

"Nothing personal. This is meant for Max."

"I don't understand," she said, stepping over debris, determined to check out what was left of her upstairs.

"It's a threat. They want to make you afraid to come home again by showing you how easy it is to get to you," he said.

"If Max testified against these guys, does that mean I'll never be safe again?" Max wouldn't be the only one who needed a new identity. "That might've been what Max was trying to tell me. I wish I'd taken his calls."

"Don't blame yourself. You couldn't have known," Jaden insisted.

Lauren sucked in a breath and kept moving. A similar scene was found on the second floor, and it angered her to the core that everything she'd worked so hard for could be destroyed in one evening. Then again, she'd only worked for *things* so far. It wasn't like she'd spent the past few hears investing in anything real. Like a family. Kids.

Lauren shook it off. She never thought of wanting those things before she met Jaden.

"We have to leave. Grab a change of clothes and anything you want from the bathroom. My place isn't far."

CHAPTER 18

LAUREN FOLLOWED Jaden's instructions without argument, still numb. She focused intently on folding and placing clothes in her overnight bag.

"What else did you learn about be in my folder?" Did it tell him how much of her life had been spent alone?

"That you're a runner. You like to jog in the morning," he said.

Her gaze trailed up to meet his. He alternated between watching the door and the window, and she was reminded how dangerous the situation was. It should be strange to be alone in her bedroom with a virtual stranger. Although, Jaden didn't feel like a stranger. Not after what they'd survived together. "What else?"

"You've been a successful entrepreneur—"

"I won't be for long. Not after I raided all the

cash." She suddenly realized she didn't leave enough to pay vendors next month. She'd taken it all. Left her entire life savings along with all the money she could secure in the middle of the sea. She heaved a deep sigh. "I *was* a successful business owner. Did that file tell you anything else about my private life?" Anger flooded her, had her asking questions before she could stop and think. "Does it say who I've dated? Who I've—"

"Slept with? No, it doesn't. Satisfied?" A flash of what looked like shame crossed his features. A pang of guilt washed over her. She was yelling at him because she couldn't yell at the real people provoking her.

Frustrated, Lauren sat down on the edge of her bed. "I'm sorry. I'm taking all this out on you. Look at you. You're hurt. You've been through everything I have and more. I shouldn't be giving you such a hard time right now."

"Believe me when I say I'm just as irritated," Jaden said, holding his position and watching the door intently.

"Of course you are. I remember you told me about your brother and how you hate all this. You must see his face in every situation," she said.

"It's more than that. This one's even more personal for me." His back teeth clenched.

"Why? What happened?"

"This bullet hole in my shoulder happened. I

attended the funeral of one of my operatives. Not two weeks later, I lost another. Then, I had to tell a wife she was going to bring up her children alone. In the past forty-eight hours I lost one damn good man on the beach and a fucking kid at my safe house." There was so much guilt and anger in those words.

"I'm so sorry, Jaden," she said. It was easy to see that he blamed himself for every loss.

He didn't immediately speak.

"How did you get shot?" She could tell this wasn't easy for him. Every muscle in his body tensed. His hands fisted and released. His lips thinned. She'd never had this much difficulty getting a few words out of him.

"Miscalculation. I trusted my partner. Smith got involved with a woman whose brother is a big time dealer in South America," he said.

"Menendez?"

He nodded. "She convinced him she was innocent. I believed her, too."

Hard to believe anyone had ever tricked a man like Jaden. Then it occurred to her why a man's judgement might slip, and a pang of jealousy rippled through her.

"Was she very beautiful?"

"Yes." His answer made Lauren wonder if that was the reason he didn't trust her back on the rocks.

She resisted asking the question she wanted answered and settled on, "What happened?"

"She walked us straight into a trap. We were supposed to meet to exchange guns for drugs. Instead, we marched into an ambush. My partner, Smith, took a bullet between the eyes. I took one to the shoulder." He nodded toward his left shoulder. She'd noticed that he'd been nursing it at times.

"And lived," she added, unable to imagine the sense of betrayal he must've felt. "You said before that all of this could be caused by someone from the inside, a mole. Why would one of your own do something like that?"

He shrugged. Anger scored his stormy blue eyes. "Why does anyone maim or murder? Greed. Sex. Power. Money."

A creak sounded on the stairs. Jaden switched gears instantly. He unlocked the safety on his weapon. "It's probably nothing. Settlement noise. But stay here while I check it out."

Lauren was used to the sound. Dallas houses were built on clay soil. And yet, hearing it after what she'd been through unnerved her just the same. She quickly finished her packing, more than ready to get out of her house.

Jaden returned a moment later. "Looks fine. We should get going, though."

"I'm ready." As they returned to the borrowed vehicle, Jaden kept a close watch all around them.

Sitting there, doing nothing but waiting for him to put her suitcase in the trunk made her feel like stink bait being dragged along the bottom of a pond full of catfish.

Her skin pricked.

Her stomach clenched.

Something felt very off but she couldn't pinpoint the reason.

Then she caught sight of a blacked-out SUV creeping along the garage.

"I see someone coming," she said, and pointed. "Over there."

Jaden stared at the vehicle for a long moment.

The tension was so thick inside the vehicle Laruen struggled to breathe. And then the SUV pulled away.

"It's fine," Jaden reassured.

"When can I see my brother?" Would she look at every SUV differently now? Would she check behind her every time she took two steps on the street?

Jaden glanced at his watch. "It's too late tonight. We'll go in the morning. Since Menendez's people seem intent on finding you we should probably change your appearance."

An urge to see for herself that Max was still okay gripped Lauren. She didn't want to wait. She was tired of waiting. What if his injuries were too great and he slipped away in the night? "What if Max doesn't—"

"He will."

She would argue the point, but Jaden had been

spot on so far. "Did Gunner say he'd let us know if anything happened to him?"

"Yes. But nothing's going to happen. He's in good hands," Jaden said.

Lauren wished she possessed the tiniest bit of his confidence.

Why did everything and everyone in Lauren's life feel so fleeting?

Jaden's home was two blocks from Laurens and had no unnecessary furniture. The living room had a couch and TV. The kitchen had a small table and chairs. There were a few dishes in the sink. The bedroom housed nothing more than a bed, and a TV tray for a nightstand. A handful of change had been tossed on top. A cord lay draped across, which looked to be a charger for his phone.

"You can put your stuff in here," Jaden said. His blue eyes darkened. "The shower's in the next room. I'd like to dress your wounds again when they're clean."

Lauren put her bag in the bedroom and moved to the bathroom where she took a hot shower. It was nice to have some comforts from home, like a razor and shaving cream.

Home?

Home had been destroyed. Like so much in her life recently. She felt emotionally wrung out and drained from inside out.

"There's food in the kitchen," Jaden said, after

knocking on the door. "I made a few phone calls. We can see Max in the morning. They'll expect us around nine."

"Did they say how he was doing?"

"Better than expected." His voice, soothing and calm, shouldn't make her feel like everything was right with the world.

It did.

The knob twisted.

"Lauren? You okay?"

"No. I'm fine," she said, allowing his deep baritone to wash over her for another minute. She was tired of fighting her feelings for Jaden. "I'll be right out."

She finished dressing in her nightshirt and pajama shorts and joined him in living room. When Jaden's gaze landed on her, appraising, heat flooded through her, and her heart stuttered.

JADEN'S PULSE hummed when he saw Lauren standing there in her sleep clothes, her fiery hair silky and flowing down her back. He was becoming painfully stiff, so he readjusted his length.

The rosy hue in Lauren's cheeks brightened.

God, she looked beautiful. He moved to her and leaned close, breathing her in. She smelled like fresh flowers and sunshine and everything good about a summer day.

When she didn't step away, blood flooded south. He smoothed his palm over her flat stomach before lowering it to grip her waist as he pulled her tightly against his bare chest. They were skin pressed against life-giving skin.

"You're beautiful," he whispered, pressing a kiss to her chin and then her lips. He dropped a hand around her hips and squeezed. "And incredibly sexy."

"Keep that up and I won't be able to stop you," she said as her bright eyes twinkled. She had eyes that he could look into for days.

She took a step back. "Jaden. We should think this through. There are probably a thousand logical reasons as to why we shouldn't sleep together."

"Who said anything about sleep?" His joke brought out the smile that sent a bolt of lightning straight to his chest.

"Do you want this? Me?" was all he asked.

A pink flush rose to her cheeks. Her gold-brown eyes darkened with desire. "Yes."

"I said we were going to finish what we started yesterday and I meant every word. But you tell me to stop and I'm hands-off." He closed the gap between them and she didn't back away. He was close enough to feel her chest rise and fall when she breathed. He felt good in this space.

Kissing the top of her shoulder, he guided his lips up the nape of her neck, across the smooth skin of her face. He feathered a kiss on the small freckle above her mouth, until his lips found hers. She parted hers and teased his tongue into her mouth.

He moved them to the bed, undressing her along the way.

His tongue, hot and needy, pressed into her mouth as she pulled him on top of her. He instinctively reacted to her movements. His passion heated with the kind of fire that had been shelved for years and finally set free.

Jaden took his time, tasking every inch of her neck, her jawline. His heft covered her, and she trembled beneath him. Her back arched and her hips shifted, her soft skin pressed against his erection.

She was perfection.

He brought up one of his hands and smoothed it across the exposed skin of her breast. Her nipple beaded and she wrapped long, lean runner's legs around his midsection.

With Lauren's naked and warm body pressed against him he noticed that she fit every part of him. The feel of her bare silky skin was enough to drive him to the brink. He thrust his tongue deep inside her mouth.

He pulled back enough to take in her body, letting his gaze linger on every curve of her incredible figure. He watched as full breasts rose and fell with every deep breath she took.

With one arm wrapped around her waist, he pulled her body tight against his before letting his hands wander over her sweet skin. He touched every inch of her stomach and then her full breasts.

Feeling the softness of the curves in her back, his hand moved lower. He slowed at the curve of her sweet bottom. The crush of fresh flowers enveloped him.

He used the tip of his tongue to click the crest of her nipple before taking it in his mouth. She moaned sexy sounds of pleasure.

Her lips quivered and her tongue darted across her perfect pink lips as his thumb grazed her beaded nipple. It was his turn to groan when he felt it swell under his touch.

"Hold that thought," he managed to say as he pushed off the bed. He disappeared into the bathroom in order to retrieve a condom, returning to Lauren quickly.

"You're beautiful," he said before his lips crushed down on hears, kicking off a whole new wave of desire as she helped him sheath his erection.

He leaned over and kissed her belly. Moved down her leg, lingering behind her knee. He brushed kisses down her calves, stopping at her ankles.

Making his way back up, he slowed at the bend of her knee before brushing his lips on the insides of her thighs. He moved his hands up the curves of her stomach, kissing his way to her earlobe.

She nuzzled against his body, kicking off a whole new swell of desire.

He splayed one hand against the small of her back, positioning her exactly where he wanted to in order to better access her silken lips. His kiss, slow and tender at first, began to deepen as she parted her lips for him.

Lauren shifted underneath him before palming his erection and guiding him inside her. He dipped his tip and the sexiest sound tore from her lips.

She bucked her hips and he surged a little deeper.

"Take me, Jaden."

CHAPTER 19

LAUREN BROUGHT her hands up to Jaden's shoulders and dug her fingers in as he thrust himself inside her. Everything about this man heightened her senses and brought her body to life. His warm and salty scent. His solid-walled chest. His beautiful blue eyes. And those lips. God those lips.

His fingers stroked her hair as she felt his lips brush her forehead, and she felt a yearning well up from deep inside that made her head numb. Being so close to him, feeling his skin under her fingers put her at war from the inside out. She struggled to do something as basic as take oxygen into her lungs as she felt his hands on her hips, and his length thrust deeper.

Lauren's body craved his touch as she moved his hands up and down his back, her fingers stopping to outline every muscle. Her senses heightened until her body pulsed and tingled with the kind of sensations that must be similar to freefalling off the face of a cliff.

She let her fingers wander, tracing his jawline and then down his chin until they mapped his muscled chest. Every part of her was awake, alive with desire, with a need to feel his bare-naked skin. His tongue marked her every curve as his, lighting a fiery trail and she couldn't imagine wanting a man more than she wanted this man.

"You're perfection," she heard him say into her thick mass of hair.

He kissed her, slowly this time, but with so much skill she got lost—lost inside him without any sense there could be anything else.

He stroked her body as his warm hand flushed a hot trail along her skin. He groaned a low, throaty growl as he stroked her breasts and she matched him thrust for thrust.

"Jaden," she managed to say.

He stopped long enough to smile at her.

Her heart was in danger.

He raised her hands above her head. He moved her to the exact position he seemed to want her, kissing her on the lips. His elbows supported his weight, kept him from crushing her.

Lauren tensed as she tightened her legs around his midsection, allowing him to drive himself home.

She brought her fingers along his muscular lines

as he thrust again. She matched his tempo. Everything was in perfect rhythm, their bodies, their breathing.

She wriggled her hips and their heat lit a fire inside her belly. "Don't stop."

"Oh, it's too late for that," he said with that devastating smile.

He pumped harder, faster, deeper.

And she met him on every level until match point. Blasts of electricity rocketed through her body. His heart pounded against her chest and his breathing was jagged as he stayed inside her, thrusting and surging until her body finished quivering and he finally let go. His breath quickened and his entire body tensed until she could feel the sweet release.

Chests heaving, he stayed on top of her until every last spasm was drained from her.

After a long moment, he rolled onto his side and pulled her against the crook of his arm.

"I'm falling for you, Jaden. But I don't even know who you are," she said quietly. She wasn't sure what she wanted to hear from him. A commitment? This soon? It sounded silly even to her. But her world had been tipped on its axis from the minute they'd met. Making love had sent her down a path there was no returning from. And a part of her needed him to know that she didn't take making love casually. "But what's the use of caring for someone when you're not even sure of his real name?"

Jaden stood, his expression darkened with hurt.

Damn his blue eyes. The pain. They had Lauren wanting to reach out to him and tell him everything would be okay. She finally understood how conflicted he was at making promises he wasn't sure he could keep.

She wanted, no needed him to speak. She craved answers she knew deep down he didn't have any more than she did.

When he didn't, she said, "You said they're expecting us in the morning. We should get sleep."

Before he could respond, she rolled over and closed her eyes.

WHY COULD Jaden speak his mind? Why couldn't he tell Lauren that everything would magically work out? There was no denying the fact that he was falling head over heels for her. What was so damn hard about speaking the words?

Instead, he sat on the edge of the bed, listening to her breathing. He told himself there was no way he could look into her eyes and lie to her. Oh, those eyes. They were the brown-gold equivalent of the North Star, bold and bright, lighting the way to his mind's salvation. They radiated acceptance, and emotion as foreign to him as love. Yet he still couldn't find his footing on the path that would take him there.

Jaden was a soldier. His world had order. He traveled most of the year. His work was dangerous. It could put her in the line of fire. She'd be a loose thread. No matter how selfish he wanted to be right then a woman like Lauren deserved so much more.

Once he heard Lauren's breathing become steady and he was certain that she'd fallen asleep, he dressed and grabbed his motorcycle helmet.

Anger fueled his footsteps out to his bike. He fired off a text to Gunner to see if his boss was still awake. Jaden's mind was churning and he needed to talk out his ideas.

Speaking of loose threads, Helena was becoming an issue.

Based on the text Jaden received while at the store, Helena was camping out on the island. Waiting.

He punched in Gunner's number as soon as he stepped outside. Jaden wanted to speak to his boss without Lauren around.

"They got to the asset's place before us. It was completely ransacked," Jaden said quickly.

"Not unexpected." Gunner's calm tone grounded Jaden. His boss was right and Jaden was getting emotionally involved. He needed distance to keep his thoughts straight.

"The way they tore the place up, I'd say they were

sending a message. Someone's angry. It felt like a threat. Could be for Max." Jaden appreciated focusing on the mission again.

"They've done their homework."

"You hear from Gabriel yet on Helena?" Jaden asked, frustrated that it had already been a month since Tim's death and they were still without any leads on the shooter.

A deep sigh came through the line. "No."

"Where does that leave us?"

"I'm afraid we can't do much of anything until we receive more data," Gunner said. "It's a watch and wait."

"You got anyone…"

"Helena, of course. Gabriel. Me and you. I don't want to involve anyone else. I'd rather keep this one under the radar and off the books."

It was probably a good call considering all that was at stake. "Wish we could contact Helena directly."

"She hasn't surfaced yet. Neither has Gabriel. With communication equipment being compromised I won't reach out to either one," Gunner said.

"She'll show up at some point." She had to. "Menendez's men were ready for us on the beach. Then, they found me and Lauren at the seaside condo. Her townhouse has been ransacked, and we had a tail not long after we touched ground." How did they anticipate his every move? The cartel had to be getting information from someone on his and

Lauren's whereabouts. The new leader, whoever he was, had raised the stakes. "We can't be too careful."

"Agreed," came quickly from Jaden's boss.

"What's the word on the brother?" Avoiding using names kept the mission less personal.

"The doctor's hopeful for a full recover." Gunner paused for a beat. "He took a beating."

Jaden needed to know what he was about to walk Lauren into come morning. "Is he conscious?"

"Unfortunately no," Gunner said.

Damn. Jaden would've liked to ask Max a few questions. "How bad does it look?"

"You saw the facial lacerations and swelling. His ribs are broken. They're running tests to determine whether or not there's internal organ damage or bleeding. They beat him within an inch of his life." Gunner's tone lowered, respectfully. Justice was one thing, but this was over the top. Which lead Jaden to believe this had been no ordinary kidnapping.

"Keep me posted on his progress," Jaden said to Gunner.

"You know I will." Gunner ended the call.

Jaden returned from the drugstore with a bag full of supplies. Lauren's russet locks would be dyed black. Jet black. Blacker than night. This would be difficult for him because he loved her long curly hair. The way waves cascaded over her shoulders. But the waves had to go.

He set the bag down and walked into the bedroom.

Instead of finding her asleep, she was sitting up and staring at a fishing magazine he'd picked up when he first came to the stakeout.

"Where'd you go?" she asked, covering the hurt in her voice by clearing her throat.

"Store. I bought a few supplies but you should—"

"Rest? I close my eyes and all I see are men with guns. I can't sleep." She threw the covers off and stood up. "Let's get this over with."

He urged her toward the kitchen in his small rented one-bedroom apartment. With her there, he realized how empty the place had been before. The feeling had no connection to the sparse decorations. It wasn't warm, like the feeling he had whenever he was near Lauren.

Then again, it wasn't meant to be. This place served a purpose, he reminded himself. Anything else would've been a distraction.

Lauren blinked up at him from the sink where he washed her hair. Her pulled scissors from the bag of supplies and cut her tresses up to her jaw line.

He somehow thought she'd look different to him. She didn't. Her pink lips were just as full. Her brown eyes just as beautiful. He washed the black color rinse in her hair, and the gold flecks in her eyes stood out even more than usual. "And what about you?"

"I have a bandana and some biker clothes in the

closet. Sunglasses and a helmet will shield my face," he said.

"Why do you really think they broke into my apartment? Would they really do all that just for a little money?"

They wanted something badly. He hoped for her sake it was information about Max. And yet, his gut told him something was wrong with the picture. Why ransack her place? Why tear it up to that degree? There was more to it. His mind wound back to it being a threat. But why?

"Do you trust Gunner?" She shocked him with the question.

"Yes." Jaden paused thoughtfully. He believed in Lauren, too.

"And you're sure?"

"If I'm wrong, I'm dead..."

She pressed a finger to his shoulder. "Screwing up in my business means a supplier doesn't get paid on time. People get upset, but no one dies."

He didn't respond. His finger flexed and released, wanting to hold her again.

"You ever think about changing your line of work?" she asked.

"No. Not until recently." He was being honest. He'd never once considered doing anything besides being a soldier.

"Because you got shot?"

He shook his head. "I—" His cell phone buzzed

before he could finish his sentence. He shot a look of apology. "I better get this."

"Gunner?"

He nodded as Lauren sucked in a breath.

"Everything okay?" Jaden asked into the phone.

CHAPTER 20

LAUREN HELD her breath waiting for news about her brother. Her heart pounded painfully against her ribs. Her gaze was glued to Jaden's face, searching for any sign, a muscle twitch that might indicate bad news.

He looped his arm around her waist. He pulled her close enough for her to hear Gunner's words. She momentarily thought about pulling away from him but her heart was all in. She sensed his might be, too, even though he'd gone quiet earlier.

"The security team is expecting you both. It should be safe. Move quickly and get out as soon as you can," Gunner said.

With her body pressed against Jaden's, she could feel his heartbeat and breathe in his musky, male scent.

As Jaden closed the phone, she felt a tender kiss press to the side of her head. "Ready?"

"Yes." Of course, she wanted to see Max, but part of her feared she wouldn't want to leave him. A thought haunted her. Soon, her brother would disappear into a new identity and she'd never see him.

Lauren couldn't imagine facing this situation alone. Guilt twisted her insides.

"It's not your fault," Jaden said, his arm wrapped around her, reassuring her, pulling her closer to him.

"I was selfish. I only thought about protecting myself instead of caring for him when I could've helped. Maybe I could've prevented all this." The thought kept replaying in her mind.

"You didn't know. You couldn't possibly have known how this situation would've turned out." Jaden's voice held no judgment, only compassion.

"With all that you went through with your brother. I'm sure you'd trade your life for the chance to see him one more time. I can tell how much you loved him." She locked gazes. "What was his name?"

"I said it before and I'll say it again. It's not your fault." Jaden paused a beat. "His name was Bobby."

Pain darkened his blue eyes.

"I'm so sorry," she said quietly, reverently.

"When someone's determined to destroy their life, you can't stop them. You were right to protect yourself." Jaden spoke with the conviction of a man who knew what he was talking about.

"I guess." She didn't argue because she wanted to get to the hospital as soon as she could. Besides, she could see it had taken a lot for Jaden to open up. And he'd closed up again just as quickly.

Lauren dressed and was ready to go inside of ten minutes.

They made it to Parkland Hospital in less than half an hour—a miracle in Dallas's morning rush hour. The hospital was known for trauma care, it had a reputation for being the best.

"I wish you'd met Max when we were kids. He had the biggest heart. He would help anyone out who needed a hand. Liking them wasn't a requirement." She handed over her helmet and Jaden secured it on the back of the motorcycle.

"Bad things can happen to good people," he said.

"You already know our dad left before I was born. Mom was a wreck. She drank too much. Brought different men in the house."

Jaden's jaw muscles clenched and his hands fisted but he said nothing.

"Max used to sleep on the floor. Right outside my door. Swore if anyone ever hurt me, he'd kill them."

"He sounds like a good brother," Jaden said, his set expression said he meant every word.

"We swore we'd never become like her." Saying those words hurt but they were true.

"Kids shouldn't be left to their own devices so

young," Jaden soothed. "The pull to the other side can become too strong without a proper anchor."

She shrugged, wiping away a tear. "He dropped out of school at thirteen, faked a birth certificate, and got a job as a dishwasher at a restaurant to put food on the table so I could stay in school. He started hanging around with older guys, a bad crowd, which lead to partying. He didn't have a chance at a normal life."

"He does now," Jaden said, pressing a tender kiss to her lips. "We'll make sure he gets the second chance he deserves."

She leaned into him. "Thank you. For everything."

Jaden linked their fingers as they headed inside the tall white hospital building.

Lauren walked into the elevator with a mix of emotions. She'd had to hold it together up until now and would have to in front of her brother, but she couldn't help but wonder what she would feel when she saw him again.

Was he the brother she remembered from childhood? The kind boy who'd taken more than his fair share of beatings for sticking up for his baby sister?

Or was he the rebellious criminal who broke her heart when he'd fallen in step with their mother?

The lab tests showed he hadn't been on drugs, and being clean was a good thing. It was a start she could build on.

They turned left, rounded the corner toward Max's room.

There were men in dark suits everywhere. Some wore business suits and had earpieces. Other wore police uniforms. Not exactly low-key but security was being taken very seriously.

As soon as Lauren took a step inside the hallway, she was stopped by one of the suits.

"This is a restricted area, ma'am."

Jaden stepped in between them. "I'm Jaden Dean, and I work for ManTech."

"Special Agent Caldwell." He stuck his hand out between them. "Pleased to meet you."

Jaden accepted a hearty-looking shake.

"I'm going to need ID, sir," Agent Caldwell said apologetically.

Jaden flashed his license. "You should also know I'm carrying."

"Sir, we'll need to search you," Caldwell countered, examining the ID.

"Understood."

Another suit came over eyeing the situation carefully. Lauren's stomach hit rock bottom. Not because her brother was being heavily guarded. That he was being so protected actually made her feel slightly better about his well-being. The level of protection he received made her stomach drop because it reminded her of how deep he'd been in and how dangerous the criminals he'd been involved with were.

Those thoughts would keep Lauren awake at night until she was certain her brother was safe. It was almost better to think he would leave this place with a fresh start. A new life. If he could bring a few jerks down in the process, better yet.

"He gave us everything we needed. Names. Locations. The people who did this to him will do hard time for the rest of their lives," the agent finally said. "He's been out ever since. Go ahead through."

Jaden's arm looped around her waist. He pulled her toward him as he led her to Max's room.

Nothing could've prepared Lauren for walking into the hospital room, seeing her brother hooked up to all those machines.

Jaden's reassuring voice rasped in her ear. "It's never as bad as it looks. He's going to be fine."

Jaden stood at the door, giving her enough space to have a private moment with her brother, yet never letting her out of his sight.

Lauren blinked back tears as she moved to Max's bedside. She sat in the chair positioned near Max's head and took his hand in hers. "Max, I'm here. It's Lauren."

Bruised and swollen, Max's eyelids fluttered.

"Get your rest, brother. I'm not leaving."

Lauren felt the hand in hers attempt to squeeze, it

was good he could hear her. His face was cut, swollen, distorted His nose was double its normal size. But it was Max. He was alive. He was getting the care he needed. And best of all, he was drug free. Soon he'd get the second chance in life he so deserved.

"You're going to be fine," she soothed.

And she hoped those words were true.

JADEN COULDN'T SHAKE the bad feeling in his bones. He was missing something, something right under his nose, and he knew it.

Lauren glanced up at him and then waved him over.

Max was straining to speak.

"I can't make out what he's saying," Lauren whispered.

Jaden had only to look into her eyes again, and he was hooked. She had him, every part of him. She'd awakened parts of his heart he'd thought long dead.

"Max is waking up," she said staring up at Jaden.

"That's good," Jaden said.

Max's eyes blinked open to slits. "It w-w-w-as herrr."

"Who?" Lauren asked intently. "Who was it, Max?"

"H-h—" He struggled to speak. "H-h-e—"

"Take your time, Max." She seemed to realize just how important his next words might be.

"H-h-he..." Max couldn't seem to drum up the energy to finish.

"What are you trying to tell us? I don't understand. Do you need me to contact someone? A friend?"

He grimaced from movement but could speak. A look of disdain darkened his swollen features. He tried to speak again, but failed.

"Don't worry, Max. I'm here. I promise I'll be here for you." The sweetness in Lauren's voice was another shot to Jaden's heart.

As Max closed his eyes again, a loud beeping sound came from his IV monitor.

"When did he wake up?" A nurse scurried into the room. Her name plate read: Serena.

"Not long." Lauren looked to Jaden. "Five minutes?"

He nodded agreement.

The machine settled, pulsing rhythmically again. Lauren issued a breath.

"You must be his sister. He perked up as soon as he heard you were coming, but he needs his rest. I'm sorry to tell you think but you need to go," Serena said.

"We just got here." Based on Lauren's slumped shoulders and deep worry lines nothing in her body language said she was ready to get up and walk out that door.

"He's been through a lot. Believe me, with the amount of pain meds he's on, he won't even remember you're here. This will all be a blur for him later." Serena stopped for a second and gave Lauren a compassionate look. "Your brother is in the best hands."

"Is there someone I can speak to about staying?" Lauren asked but Jaden realized the battle was lost before it had been fought.

"You can take it up with administration. Won't do any good. Not on this floor. I'm sorry. I can see you love your brother very much. I know you want what's best for him. He needs rest if he's going to get better. You do, too. His recover is going to be a marathon, honey." Serena's compassion seemed to strike a chord with Lauren.

There was no way Jaden would tell her to leave. But he could see the argument playing out in her mind. She didn't want to leave but the last thing she wanted was to get in the way of his healing.

Jaden leaned into her ear. "He knows you're here. We can come back tomorrow."

"Promise?" Her hopeful eyes nearly gutted him.

"Yes. As soon as they open the doors and give us the okay." Jaden didn't do promises but this was Lauren. And nothing would stop him from coming through for her.

Serena, who had been fidgeting with knobs, rocked her head. "He's on a strict schedule. His visitation is so restricted I'm surprised you got through today. But come back tomorrow. It never hurts to keep trying until you wear them down."

The nurse winked at Lauren, who returned with a tearful smile.

"Thank you," she said.

"Let's grab lunch," Jaden said to Lauren.

It was clear that Lauren didn't want to leave. Jaden understood that seeing her brother in this condition must be difficult but not as hard as facing the thought of leaving him twice. The thought that her brother could disappear at any moment into Witness Protection was probably weighing heavily on her mind.

Serena, looking sympathetic, said, "Look, I'll speak to the doctor and see if we can get you some extra time tomorrow."

"You can't know what that would mean to me," Lauren said gratefully.

Jaden's hand never left her back as they walked out. She eased onto the back of the motorcycle, wrapped her arms around him and leaned her face against his back. He didn't pit stop on the way home. He kept going until they returned safely to his place.

"Just remember he's going to be fine," he said once they were back inside.

"He was trying to tell me something and I

couldn't make it out." Lauren's hands worked the ends of a pillow as she sat on the sofa.

"Maybe we'll get another chance to talk to him tomorrow. I know he looks bad to you right now, but believe me when I say that I've seen a lot worse," Jaden tried to offer reassurance as he took a seat next to her.

"Like your injuries?" She brought her hand up to his shoulder with the bullet hole.

"That's nothing." She tensed when he said what was supposed to reassure her.

Lauren's finger traced the rough skin, the scars covering what had been a hole in his shoulder. She brushed a kiss there. "This woman you trusted, did the two of you get very close?"

"Not this close," he said and his lips found hers.

Jaden knew all too well this feeling of the world being right for just a second wouldn't last.

CHAPTER 21

LAUREN LAY SLEEPING in Jaden's bed, his protective arms encircling her. Her steady, even breathing said she was asleep. She'd managed to get a few bites down before another round of the best sex of Jaden's life.

She stirred a place deep inside him—a place that had lain dormant forever—a place that made him want to protect her, to do whatever it took to keep her safe and happy, to tell her all his secrets.

His first instinct was to fight the feeling.

Not wanting to get inside his head about what that meant, how it all would work, he focused on what he knew. He wanted to be with her.

Something about the case bothered him. His thoughts circled back to Lauren. The same question haunted him. Why did they seem so intent on involving her?

He was overlooking something. A connection or link he hadn't thought of already. Who else was connected to Lauren? Looking at her, their bodies linked, a thought struck. Him. He was the only person, aside from Max, she was connected to.

Hells bells.

Couldn't be. What if the cartel had been trying to ferret out Jaden? But why? What was Max trying to tell them? He'd repeated "Herrr."

The realization hit Jaden like a jackhammer to his solar plexus. Herrrr was a woman. Helena? Now his worst fears might be playing out that Helena was behind this.

When he really thought about it everyone around her dropped like napalm. Why hadn't he pieced this together before? The hollow look in her eyes the day of Tim's funeral had haunted Jaden. Something broke in her the day she'd lost him. What if Helena was never after Max or Lauren. She was using them to get to Jaden. Why? Did she blame him for Tim's death? That would make this personal.

She was focused on the man with the angel tattoo and Jaden.

Guilt hit him fast and hard, rolling his insides. Lauren might be safe by now if not for him. One of the Menendez boys must've identified Jaden on the beach.

It felt like the worst kind of betrayal lying next to

Lauren, having her feel his protection, when, in fact, she could be in more danger because of him.

Icy fingers squeezed his heart. Jaden slid out of the covers, snatched his cell from the makeshift bedside table, pulled on a pair of jeans, and slipped out the front door.

Was Gabriel still with Helena? He texted him. Nothing. He called Gunner next. No answer.

Wishing he had a friend to talk to had him thinking of his old buddy, Tate "Bear" Parker. But, damn, it had been a long time since the two had talked. Jaden knew that Bear had been medically discharged from the Army and was now working in Montana for the Brotherhood Protectors as a body-guard. The last Jaden had heard, Bear had found what sounded like the real deal with a screenwriter by the name of Mia.

Good for him.

The private agency job he'd taken in Montana seemed to make him happy. Jaden had some serious contemplating to do. Could he set up his own shop in Texas? Bring in a few good men? Help others and know who the hell he was fighting and what they were fighting for? No more black ops. No more secrets. It gave him a lot to think about. Living life on his own terms sounded damn good about now.

A former D-Force soldier, Bear had lost most of his men when an Iraqi informant double crossed them. If not for the close air support that had been called in, Bear wouldn't be alive right now. He'd had a long road to recovery after taking a hit to his leg, but the last time the two talked Bear sounded like a new man.

Out of desperation, Jaden called his former friend. A true handyman, Bear could fix just about anything. Could he fix this? Fix Jaden?

As Jaden always did, he sent a coded text first.

"Hey." Bear picked up on the first ring.

"It's good to hear your voice, bro," Jaden said.

"Are you about to ask me on a date?" Bear teased. Jaden missed the easy way he had with his former friend.

"Yeah, why? Have you gone all exclusive now with Mia?"

"How'd you kno—" Bear stopped midsentence. He chuckled again, realizing he wasn't exactly incognito in Montana and he was having a conversation with basically a ghost. "Never mind that. I'm sure you have your ways. What's going on?"

"Does something have to be up for me to reconnect with an old friend?" Jaden's comeback fell flat.

There was silence on the line.

"We have a mole." Jaden dove right in.

"Shit. Do you know who it is?"

"I think so," Jaden admitted. "The problem is, she's one of our best."

"Then you have to do whatever it takes to bring her out of the shadows." Bear was right. Jaden could only think of one way to do that but damn it was dangerous...

His cell buzzed in his hand. He moved it away from his ear and checked the screen. Gunner.

"I have to take this one." Jaden cursed the timing.

"Sure, I understand. You need any help out there wherever you are?"

Jaden figured he had to handle this one. "No. I got this. But, Bear..."

"Yeah?"

"Think we could grab a beer sometime?"

"I'd like that a lot."

"Keep your eye on the news if you want to find me." Jaden didn't say goodbye. That word was too hard for him lately. He clicked over to answer the call coming in.

"Have you heard from Gabriel?" Jaden wasted no time asking.

"No."

"Get men on it. He's in danger. I'm afraid that I know who is behind all this. I think I know who's calling the shots." Jaden paused. "You're not going to like this. I think it's Helena. When you think about it, it makes perfect sense. She's working with Menendez to draw out the man responsible for killing Tim and focusing on Lauren because I got the assignment."

Jaden's accusation was met with silence.

Then came, "Why you?"

"I gave him that assignment and now everyone around me has been shot. She's using Menendez as a cover, infiltrating them to get close to the guy with the angel tattoo. She blames me for Tim's death. Hell, I do, too. He was all she had. She tried to kill me when I was on assignment with Smith. When she didn't succeed, she knew I'd be on my guard this time even more. She also knew I'd take an easy assignment while I healed and probably had access to the assignments in the database."

"She got to the intel before I made it disappear. She's been using the Menendez cartel as a front." Regret laced Gunner's tone as he caught on.

"This started with me, and it ends with me. I have a plan. I'll need your help," Jaden said.

"Name it."

Jaden relayed a few details before closing the phone. His chest was heavy as his thoughts snapped to his biggest issue—a problem he didn't want to face. If Helena kidnapped Max so she could target Lauren in order to draw Jaden out, the only way to keep her safe would be to distance himself from her.

To leave her.

A knife stabbed his chest. This was going to hurt far worse than a bullet to the heart. She'd awakened a place in him he thought was long dead. Now that it was awake, he couldn't imagine the pain involved in shutting it down.

Jaden walked inside the apartment, woke her and sat on the edge of the bed.

Lauren took one look at his serious expression and sat straight up. "What's wrong?"

She tried to touch him, but he pulled on all his strength and moved out of reach. "Gunner set up a safe house for you. You'll be watched day and night. An agent will be here to pick you up in a few minutes."

"And what about you?" She was pulling on her strength not to break down. He'd heard it in her voice before when she'd been talking about Max.

"I have a new assignment." It wasn't a lie. His mission had changed.

"So that's it then. You ride off into the sunset, and don't look back?" she asked bitterly.

"Look. It's work. It's what I do." He needed her to believe that he could walk away even though it was killing him inside.

"Fine. Do what you have to." She turned her face away from him.

Jaden stood up, dropped an envelope full of cash on the nightstand and then walked out.

Losing her forever was something he couldn't fathom. He lied to himself, saying he'd see her again. In truth, he knew she'd never want to look at his face again after the way he'd just hurt her.

Jaden fired up his motorcycle engine, forcing his thoughts to what was important. She was safe now.

Anger burned through his lungs, making something as simple as taking in air painful.

What else could he do? Wheels were in motion. He had to sort out his thoughts, clear his focus, so he made damn sure no one would hurt her again.

Besides, he couldn't concentrate when her body was pressed against his. Not even a holy man could resist that kind of temptation.

He was no saint.

No threat he'd be called up for that job anytime soon, either.

And right now?

He was a bastard instead.

By the time Lauren settled into the safe house, her body was nearing exhaustion. Alone was how she came into the world, and alone was how she'd probably leave. Life had a way of charting a course.

The apartment in the top floor of a downtown building was cozy, comfortable. Leather club chairs flanked an ottoman across from an exposed brick fireplace. An armoire in the corner encased a TV and DVDs. Save for the man parked outside her door, this felt as close to home as anything could, under the circumstances.

But without Jaden, even home seemed hollow.

All she could think about was a hot bath, candlelight, and a tall glass of wine. Arranging all her props, Lauren stepped into the bath water. She eased in and practically glided down the back of the tub.

In the warmth, her physical aches and pains melted into the water. The emotional ones wouldn't wash away so easily. She exhaled slowly to clear her mind. No pressure. No outside distractions. She was alone with her thoughts. They wandered to Jaden first.

Her heart tore in half from missing him so much. She could scarcely breathe.

She reminded herself that she'd known all along this was going to happen. But it sure hurt like hell.

A full hour later, she stood, rinsed off, and put on pajamas. Curling up in bed, the distant rumble of a thunderstorm comforted her. She missed Jaden's arms around her.

He'd made a life out of being on his own. Is that why he'd pushed her away?

An annoying voice reminded her that Max was safe now. Jaden had completed this mission and was on to the next. It hurt. And a question swirled around in her head, keeping her from sleep. Why did he push her away now?

Lauren fell asleep as the rains came, thunder and lightning cracking against the sky.

When she checked the clock the next morning,

she realized she'd slept nearly twelve hours. Her thoughts slammed to Jaden. He'd been the one to teach her the lesson looping through her thoughts. *You can't change someone who doesn't want to change.*

Lauren slipped out onto the tiny patio. The noon sun was already overhead. Her newly-minted black hair whipped around in a rare cool summer breeze.

When she was sufficiently awake and grounded, she decided to plug back into life and watch the news. Maybe she could catch up a bit while she got ready for work. The flower shop was closed but she needed to get in there and assess the financial damage. See if there was anything left to save of her business. She slipped on jeans and a t-shirt.

One glance at the TV and she froze.

"An operative, known as Jaden Dean, linked to a secret organization called ManTech is speaking out against evil."

Her pulse climbed. Lauren raced to the set, cranked up the volume. Why would he do this? Why would he blow his cover?

"The ex-special forces operative not only gives away his identity, but he delivers a call to action in this YouTube video, which is going viral on the Internet…" the broadcaster continued.

Lauren blinked hard as the homemade video came up on the screen, featuring a man who unmistakably Jaden.

"This is Jaden Orchard. The company I work for

has been infiltrated by a South American cartel. Our operatives are being killed on assignment left and right. If you're listening, assholes, you missed one. Me. You tried and failed. You want me? Come get me. I'm here in Caracas at the Parque Carabobo subway station, and I'm waiting for you."

CHAPTER 22

LAUREN'S HEART dropped to the floor. Why would he do this? Why was he exposing himself? Taunting them. Why would he say his real name?

The shot in the video panned out to reveal several red tables and stools with men playing chess against the backdrop of what looked like a subway hub. They'd find him and kill him. What was he doing?

The doorbell rang.

Lauren answered quickly, fearing there'd be news about something happening to Jaden.

"Ma'am, it's shift change. I need you to wait here while we secure the perimeter," Dewey Burton, her night shift guard, said before disappearing down the hall.

Her nerves were fried. She couldn't stop thinking about Jaden. He'd blasted his location to the world. Sitting there, waiting, made it worse.

But she'd be crazy to take off by herself, so she waited.

Once Granger Roxbury—a.k.a. Rocky—showed, she walked past him with a greeting and took off toward her shop. He must've picked up on her mood because he gave her space. She needed a minute to breathe, anyway.

On the walk to her shop, anxiety caused her knees to shake and her shoulders to slump forward. Her knuckles felt like they would bruise from dragging the pavement. Every step was a chore. She was tired. The physical bruises pounded and she was starting to rack up emotional ones of a similar scale.

Why would he do it? Why would he push her away and then go to Caracus to expose his identity?

A sudden thought hit her. If Jaden's feelings had been real—and she knew in her heart they were—what if he'd pushed her away for her own good? He'd said he would do anything to keep her safe. Did that include forcing her away to reveal his own identity?

Try as he did to hide his true feelings, the pained expression he wore before he walked away tipped off his real emotions.

Another thought occurred to her. When she'd visited Max other day, he'd said "Herrr." A woman. Was it the one Jaden had mentioned? The woman who'd betrayed him?

Frustration climbed up Lauren's throat causing a heated rash. How could she find him now even if she wanted to? He was on another continent. He was making himself a sitting duck for professionally trained killers.

Lauren opened her shop, needing to focus on work to take her mind off Jaden. She had no cell number to use to reach him and there was nothing she could do about it. She flipped on the light switch, but nothing happened. A breaker had probably been tripped. The thunderstorm last night was the likely culprit.

"It's probably a breaker," she said to Rocky. "It'll only take a second to fix it."

There was enough light in the shop to see him nod. He moved to a position at the door and folded his arms. She pulled the emergency flashlight out from behind the counter, set down her keys, and moved to the stock room.

It didn't take but a minute to locate the box. Power outages during storms were becoming more and more common in Texas, and Lauren knew far too much about how the power box worked at her shop because of them.

The door chimed out front. She froze. And then she remembered that she had Rocky. Relief washed over her. Plus, she had lights now. She moved from the storeroom quickly and back out onto the floor.

"Rocky?" The man was short but thick—thick arms, thick neck. He was nothing but muscle and hard to misplace. She didn't see anyone else, either.

Her heart skipped a beat, her thoughts snapped back to Jaden. But that was impossible. Jaden was in Caracas. He was miles and miles away. He would not be there, in her flower shop.

Rocky probably stepped out front.

"Anyone here?" she asked, scanning the racks. She didn't see anyone and the blinds were still closed out front. If Rocky had stepped out he'd be impossible to see from this vantage point. She'd feel better if she locked the door.

Maybe she could get his attention, ask him to come back in. Lauren glanced around for the keys. She remembered them being on the counter.

Lauren moved to the cash register and looked around, but they weren't there. She searched the area, the counter and the floor. She located them between the register and the wall.

As she turned toward the door, she saw a figure move behind a rack. Lauren froze. Her heart stuttered. A little gasp escaped her before she could swallow it. Where was Rocky?

Someone was there, messing with her. Impossible as it was, her heart wanted it to be Jaden. "Who is it? Who's there?"

There was no answer. Her stomach knotted because she feared something bad had happened to Rocky. Jaden's words came back to her. Whenever in danger use anything from her surroundings to defend herself.

Sticking near the front of the shop was her best opportunity to escape. With her back to the door, she fisted the key ring, allowing the jagged edges of the keys to poke through her balled fingers. It wasn't much, but they were the only weapons she had.

Fear and panic welled in her throat. She stifled a cough. The room was quiet. Tense. It was a stalemate.

Lauren heard the squeak of a dressing room door opening. She ventured a few steps toward the door. If she could get to the front of her shop maybe she could get to the street.

From seemingly nowhere she felt a blow to the back of her head, and something heavy smacked against her back. She stumbled a few steps forward, blurry-eyed, but managed to stay on her feet. A rope pulled tightly against her neck, and a white cloth covered her mouth.

There was something on the rag. A strong odor. It wasn't a scent she could identify, but it was screaming at her. She held her breath and fought against the nausea burning her throat. She jabbed her arm backward.

The person behind her was smaller in stature. A strong elbow to the ribs might give Lauren the break she needed. She jammed her elbow into the woman behind her. The grip loosened.

Lauren took advantage of the change in momentum. She spun around and then pushed off the woman. It was a woman. A blond woman. Helena.

The door chimed as a punch landed on Lauren's solar plexus. Air flew from her lungs with an audible whoosh. The voice she thought she'd never hear again cut through the ringing sound in her ears.

"I'm the one you want. Leave her alone, Helena," said Jaden, his voice angrier than she'd ever heard it before.

The next blow dropped Lauren to her knees. Before she could scream, a strong hand guided her upright again and Helena took a couple of steps back. The barrel of her shiny gun trained on Lauren's chest.

"You came back for this one. Just as I knew you would. I saw the way you looked at her in Antigua. Did you think I would not hunt you?" the newly-blonde Helena said, her honey-coated Latin accent couldn't hide the bite in her words, the venom on her tongue.

"She has nothing to do with this," Jaden said, bitterness deepening his tone as he stood between Lauren and Helena.

The blonde's eyes twinkled, and her lips turned up in a sarcastic grin. "You like this one. Is Jaden Dean, excuse me, is Jaden Orchard finally in love? Then you're about to know what it's like for the one person you love to die."

"You don't need her to make your point. You found me. I promise you won't kill me."

Helena's cat eyes stayed intent on Jaden. "Don't be so sure."

Jaden's grip tightened on his gun. "It won't bring him back."

She let out a pained screech.

"You keep slipping out of sight, you sonofabitch. You won't do it this time," Helena said before disappearing behind a rack filled with pots.

"I mourn his loss too. Your head's not on straight. We can get help for you, Helena. It doesn't have to be this way."

"Don't pretend to be my friend. You killed him. You're in charge. You're the guy who decides where we go and when," her tone more desperate than before.

"I'm responsible for Tim. I'll take that blame. I would've gone myself if I'd known what was going to happen."

"You sent him to his death." Her voice was a screech.

"Sent him? I didn't have to. He begged me to go," Jaden said.

"Liar!"

"You didn't know? He wouldn't take no for an answer. Said he wanted to earn extra time off."

"We were supposed to be married." Her pitch rose in anger.

Jaden spun around to the sound of her every

move, protective of Lauren, who he'd tucked behind him. "Where's Gabriel?"

A bullet pinged off the metal clothing rack next to her head. In one swoop, Jaden had her on the floor, using his body to cover her.

"Gone."

Damn it. He encouraged Lauren to inch forward as he scanned the floor for Helena's feet. She was most likely using the cash register station for cover. He squeezed the handle of his Glock. Waited. The last thing he wanted to do was use it on her.

A creak from the wood floor sounded by the door. Jaden tracked the noise with the barrel of his gun. He glanced at the wall of mirrors and caught sight of Helena coming up from behind.

He spun around as she moved into his line of fire. He hesitated.

The barrel of her gun pointed directly at Lauren. He quickly adjusted so that Lauren was behind him and he had Helena in sight.

One shot. One kill.

Jaden's finger twitched on the trigger.

CHAPTER 23

JADEN COULDN'T BRING himself to shoot Helena. She was one of theirs and he'd taken an oath to protect his own. Besides, he blamed himself for this situation. He should've seen what was happening with Helena. He should've insisted she take time off or ordered therapy. He should've done a better job of taking care of her after she'd lost Tim. He'd looked into her eyes at the funeral. He'd seen how lost she'd been.

The brief hesitation cost him the advantage. Helena disappeared.

Jaden bit out a curse. He needed a new plan because Helena would shoot Lauren in order to make him suffer.

He'd lost visual with her so he needed to bring her out again.

Luring her, he made sure she heard the door click

as he slipped inside the dark storeroom. Light spilled into the room as she followed. She obviously wanted to take him out badly to expose herself like that. Jaden could use that against her.

He tucked Lauren behind a row of boxes in dead silence. He pulled his cell from his pocket, texted Gunner to alert local police. Rocky was outside, unconscious. He needed medical attention.

A long strip of cord found its way into his hand. Lauren's doing. She knew this storeroom and where her supplies were. When he was sure she'd made it back to her hiding spot safely, he stepped into a box and knocked it over so his location would be compromised.

He could feel Helena closing in.

The light flipped on as Lauren screamed.

"Now, you're going to watch her die," Helena said. Her shrill voice sounded like someone different.

"No one else dies because of me, Helena," he stated with all the authority he could.

"An eye for an eye."

"She didn't do anything to you. Would Tim want you to take an innocent life?" Helena knew the answer. Tim would never have wanted this. He was a decent man and brave soldier. He would never want an innocent person to suffer.

Her moment of hesitation was all he needed. He dove into her, knocking the gun from her hand.

Lauren scrambled to her feet and ran out of the storeroom.

Helena's fists came flying at him, connecting with his face, his chest. He grabbed her hands, located the cord, and tied them behind her back.

"You bastard. It's your fault he's gone," she seethed.

"I know."

"My life is over." She yanked her arms, trying to break the bindings but they were too tight.

"Not if I have anything to say about it," Jaden said.

"Kill me. I don't want to live without him." The anguish in her voice told him that she wasn't lying.

"I know."

Tears flooded her cheeks as her shoulders quaked. "I don't want to live…" Sobs echoed through the back room.

"I know. But it'll get better. We'll get you the help you need." He kept his voice as calm as he could.

"Why? I don't deserve it. I tried to kill you. Why would you help me?" she asked.

"Like it or not, you're my family now. And I won't turn my back on you." He wasn't sure if his words got through or not, but he would ensure she got the help she needed. "You're not one of them. You're one of the good guys. What did you do with Gabriel?"

Helena's blank eyes stared forward.

"Tim wouldn't want this."

A flicker of anguish crossed her features. "At headquarters. Tied up."

A tsunami of relief washed over Jaden. He immediately texted the news to Gunner.

Within moments, a squad car appeared, complete with the blare of sirens and flashing lights.

Lauren stood, watching it all, not really comprehending any of it based on her stony expression. Rocky was loaded into an ambulance. His face had lacerations but he would pull through just fine.

Jaden kept a close eye on Helena until military authorities arrived. Helena would outsmart local police and be free in time for dinner if they tried to contain her. Jaden couldn't have that.

When Helena was bound and placed into the back of an SUV, Jaden turned his full attention to Lauren.

"Rocky will be fine," he reassured.

"How'd you get here? It's impossible. No one can be in two places at once. I saw you on the news," she said and her voice was even, emotionless.

Jaden couldn't tell if she was glad to see him. He'd have to wait for her to regain her senses to know if she'd ever forgive him for pushing her away. "Computer trick. Gunner and I came up with it."

Almost out of thin air, when his name was said, Gunner appeared. "A crew is on the way to pick up Gabriel at headquarters. Everyone okay here?"

"Not everyone," said Jaden, motioning toward the sobbing Helena in the back of the SUV.

"I'm sorry," He said to Jaden.

"Me, too." He turned to Lauren, to the light.

Men in uniform were everywhere. Her precious business was being marked as a crime scene. She seemed in shock.

Jaden took the keys from her and locked up. He guided her back to the safe house where she'd be more comfortable. Had he gone too far in pushing her away before? He'd had to be convincing. Her life had depended on it.

His heart was ready to burst from one of his own betraying him. Didn't change the fact Tim was dead because of him. Guilt slammed into him in knowing he'd failed his own.

He would not survive the shitstorm of guilt without Lauren by his side as his equal, his best friend...the love of his life. But he'd ruined that, too.

Could she forgive him?

Once she'd showered and changed, she looked a little more settled in reality. She emerged from the bedroom in perfect timing since Jaden had just finished pouring a cold beer for himself and a glass of wine for her.

He feared the worst. She might never let him back in her life.

He had to know for sure.

Jaden pulled her toward him and leaned in until his forehead rested against hers.

She smelled clean, a mix of fresh flowers and soap and everything good in the world.

Guiding dark locks of hair behind her ear, he ran the back of his forefinger down her arm. Her body quivered with his touch. At least she still reacted to him physically. God, her skin was soft. Her eyes wide. Those beautiful golden eyes. She was the light.

Lauren pulled back, and his heart stuttered. Fear that he'd blown it overwhelmed him.

Jaden Orchard had never been afraid of anything. Until now.

"You blew your cover. Does that mean you'll be finding a new job? Maybe sticking around this time?" she asked, not giving away her true emotions.

He couldn't be so close to her without touching her. He brought his hand up to her face, and he guided her lips within an inch of his. She didn't fight him.

Was it even possible to hope she'd figured it all out? Did he still have a chance?

His voice was low, husky, when he whispered, "Are you sure you want this? Me? I'm far from perfect."

"I need real."

"This is real." He kissed her. "I'm real."

He finally pulled back and searched her eyes.

"That's exactly what I want. *You.*"

His heart practically burst. "Then let's make it official. Marry me."

He looked into her eyes like he was issuing a dare. And then bent down on one knee. "I love you. I don't want to spend another minute without you. Being away the last twenty-four hours was worse than death. I don't ever want to leave you again. I want to make this permanent. I want you to be my wife."

Her expression was unreadable when she asked, "Your real name Jaden Orchard?"

"Yes," he confirmed.

"Then who would I be marrying? Jaden Orchard or Jaden Dean?"

"Both. But I haven't been Jaden Orchard in a long time. Does the name on the wrapper matter? It's still me. The man who can't get enough of you."

"It doesn't make a difference to me. I was just wondering if I'd be Lauren Orchard or Lauren Dean," she said, and she finally smiled. "I love you, Jaden. I knew by the end of the first day with you that my heart was in big trouble. I want to spend the rest of my life with you. I've never been more certain of anything in my life. You're my home."

Her words were pure sunshine on his heart.

"If you marry me, I'll let you pick our last name and we'll find a way to protect your brother and keep the two of you in touch. You don't have to lose anyone again. As for us, we can be whoever you want. How about that?" He kissed her again, soft and tender.

"Yes, Jaden. I will marry you."

His chest swelled with pride when he heard the word *yes*. It was the only thing that mattered. Everything else could be figured out along the way.

Jaden swept Lauren off her feet, buried his face in her hair, and then carried her toward the bedroom.

"I hope you plan to be here for a while," she said, and her eyes glittered with need.

He looked into those beautiful eyes and saw forever.

"Sweetheart, I never plan to leave."

EPILOGUE

DANIEL DAMON SAT on a limb high in the old oak at the edge of the Katy Trail playground, watching his five-year-old daughter play. He twisted his wedding ring around his finger a couple of times.

A man should know what to say to his daughter, to his wife.

Daniel came up empty. He was a soldier before becoming an operative. He'd been damn good at both jobs. And he hadn't been home for longer than a seven-day stretch in more than six years.

Staring at his family, he didn't have the first idea how to approach them with the news that Daddy was coming home. The Blackwater-type agency he'd spent the past three years working for after serving his country had literally just imploded.

The agency had been compromised. He'd received the code no one at ManTech ever wanted. Gunner, the owner, had issued the Code Eighty-Six after one of its female operatives admitted to putting names and faces out on the dark Web. No one knew for certain if what she said was true. It wouldn't matter.

Now that word was out that ManTech had been infiltrated, no government agency in the world would hire them.

For the first time in his adult life Daniel was out of a job.

He almost laughed out loud. A job? Being a soldier and then an operative had been his life.

And he had no clue what he was going to do next.

In Hero's Junction, Colorado, Ash Cage tries to put the military, his home state of Texas and the past behind him working as a handyman despite nerve damage to his right hand. His plate is full since taking on retired military dog "Seven" who would've had a much worse fate if left to the military. Even so, Ash is starting to get his bearings in the civilian world. Until his life is turned upside-down once again when he comes to the aid of a beautiful car crash victim on the run from a killer.

ABOUT BARB HAN

Barb Han is a USA TODAY, Publisher's Weekly, and Amazon Bestselling Author. Reviewers have called her books "heartfelt" and "exciting."

She lives in Texas—her true north—with her adventurous family, a poodle mix and a spunky rescue who is often referred to as a hot mess. She is the proud owner of too many books (if there is such a thing). When not writing, she can be found exploring Manhattan, on a mountain either hiking or skiing depending on the season, or swimming in her own backyard.

Sign up for Barb's newsletter at www.BarbHan.com.

BROTHERHOOD PROTECTORS

ORIGINAL SERIES BY ELLE JAMES

Brotherhood Protectors Series

Montana SEAL (#1)

Bride Protector SEAL (#2)

Montana D-Force (#3)

Cowboy D-Force (#4)

Montana Ranger (#5)

Montana Dog Soldier (#6)

Montana SEAL Daddy (#7)

Montana Ranger's Wedding Vow (#8)

Montana SEAL Undercover Daddy (#9)

Cape Cod SEAL Rescue (#10)

Montana SEAL Friendly Fire (#11)

Montana SEAL's Mail-Order Bride (#12)

SEAL Justice (#13)

Ranger Creed (#14)

Delta Force Strong (#15)

Montana Rescue (Sleeper SEAL)

Hot SEAL Salty Dog (SEALs in Paradise)

Hot SEAL Hawaiian Nights (SEALs in Paradise)

ABOUT ELLE JAMES

ELLE JAMES also writing as MYLA JACKSON is a *New York Times* and *USA Today* Bestselling author of books including cowboys, intrigues and paranormal adventures that keep her readers on the edges of their seats. With over eighty works in a variety of sub-genres and lengths she has published with Harlequin, Samhain, Ellora's Cave, Kensington, Cleis Press, and Avon. When she's not at her computer, she's traveling, snow skiing, boating, or riding her ATV, dreaming up new stories. Learn more about Elle James at www.ellejames.com

Website | Facebook | Twitter | GoodReads | Newsletter | BookBub | Amazon

Follow Elle!
www.ellejames.com
ellejames@ellejames.com

facebook.com/ellejamesauthor
twitter.com/ElleJamesAuthor

CPSIA information can be obtained
at www.ICGtesting.com
Printed in the USA
LVHW080005220621
690817LV00024B/985